FATED TO THE GRIZZLY

OBSESSED MOUNTAIN MATES

ARIANA HAWKES

D1736058

Imprint: Independently published

ISBN: 9798324444914

Cover art: Thunderface Design

www.arianahawkes.com

1

Scout

I'm sitting in the back of a battered old truck with screwed suspension. My dad is at the wheel, I'm blindfolded, and my two older brothers are sitting on either side of me.

This might make more sense if I explain that I was raised in a cult.

I know, I know. You're probably thinking polygamy. Praying to some creepy dude in a toga. Extreme yoga. It's not *that* kind of cult.

My family are preppers. We belong to a whole community known as *The Emergency Preparedness Brotherhood*, who are awaiting the *Final Fiasco*.

Fifty percent of my dad's conversation involves speculating over what the Final Fiasco might entail. Spoiler: some real bad, scary shit.

The other fifty percent is focused on how the heck we can protect ourselves from it.

I first figured out there was something "atypical" about my family when my bestie, Casey, and I were about eleven, and I took her down to my family's basement.

"Dude, this is unreal," she breathed, wandering among the rows of shelves stacked with every possible type of non-perishable item. Enough instant noodles to feed a small army; meticulously labeled bins of dried beans, rice, and grains; towering monoliths of canned ravioli, baked beans, tuna, Easy Mac. A fortress of energy drinks, and the pièce de resistance—a giant pyramid of toilet paper.

I shrugged. "It's just our stock."

She turned to me. "That's a lot of stock, Scout."

I planted my hands on my hips proudly. "We gotta be ready for the end of times."

"The what?" I saw something new in her eyes then— a flicker of alarm.

"What do *you* store in your basement?"

She frowned. "You've seen our basement. It's just a den. We have couches and a big TV."

"But where's your *stock*?"

"On a couple of shelves in the kitchen, I guess."

"And that's all you have?"

"Uh huh." Her gaze flickered to the door that led out of the basement.

My stomach turned over. My dad had warned me about *The Unprepared*. They were going to be some of our biggest enemies when the *Final Fiasco* came, because, having failed to protect themselves, they would try to steal all our stock.

I fixed her with a serious look. "Casey, it's real important you stock up—"

She frowned. "Quit being weird, Scout."

She wasn't getting it. I had to make her see. She was my best friend and I loved her. I grabbed her by the shoulders. "You'll all starve to death, and it's not gonna be pretty. At all," I screamed, using one of my dad's favorite expressions.

Her eyes filled with fear and she yanked herself out of my grasp. "I've gotta go help my mom out with some chores," she said, fast-walking toward the exit. I watched her go, pulsating with pity and fear.

After that, things just got worse. At school, I volunteered to lead a fire drill, and instructed everyone to dive under their desks and "combat-crawl" to the nearest exit. Then I brought my hand-cranked emergency radio to show-and-tell. Everyone laughed their asses off when I accidentally picked up a truck driver's karaoke sing-along, complete with a falsetto version of *I Will Survive*. Then I set off the metal detectors at the entrance gates with the sheer number of safety pins in my emergency kit...

The list of humiliations goes on and on.

Honestly, it was a relief when my dad took my big brothers and me out of school and home schooled us instead.

But after a couple of years, prepping in an urban environment wasn't enough for him, and he dragged us all off to live in the middle of a forest in an underground bunker. Off-grid of course, and a million miles from civilization.

And I hate it. It's been eight long years of chopping firewood, wondering if those mushrooms I just foraged are gonna take us all out, and skinning and disemboweling small animals. I'm not cut out for wilderness life. At all.

See our name, *Brotherhood*. It's all about dudes. Being outdoorsy. Wrestling. Having burping contests after biting the heads off raw lizards. That kinda shit.

I like nice things: scented candles, manicures, lattes. A nice soft bed to lie down in after a day spent scrubbing clothes in a stream. I'm a typical girl; so sue me. And it's sure lonely. My mom is no support, either. Over the years, she's kinda faded. Trying to feed a family of five in the wilderness takes so much out of her, she's always exhausted, and she accepts my father's crazy ideas and directives without argument.

I try not to be mad at her. My dad is a real forceful personality. And when he gets that glint in his eye, it's best to just do whatever he wants.

WHICH BRINGS me to my current predicament. A week ago, I turned twenty-one, and dad decided there's no time like his daughter coming of age to foster closer relations with other members of the Brotherhood.

So, he offered me to the eldest son of a neighboring family.

Yes, you heard that right.

The day after my birthday, he told me to pick out my

best outfit from the bunch of rags that pass for my clothes these days. He also said, "comb your hair, for christsakes."

Which was a bit rich, since he'd banned us from bringing anything to our forest home that wasn't a tool for weathering the *Final Fiasco*, and hairbrushes sure didn't make the cut.

Still, over the years, I've figured out which plants I can mash together to create some kind of shampoo and detangling conditioner, and I did my best to make my hair look presentable.

Then, with his typical dad habit of keeping everything on a "need to know basis," he disappeared for a while, and returned with the truck I thought he'd sold long ago.

He bundled me into the back of it and drove me to meet my suitor.

Every terrible moment of the episode is emblazoned on my brain forever.

The Gaskills are a different kind of family from ours. Not that I'm an expert on the subject, but they have less of dad's doomsday-obsessed intensity, and more of an anti-government militia vibe. To be honest, I think dad was hoping to benefit from their muscle.

But when dad dumped a flower garland on my head —probably made by my mom—and shoved me through their front door, their son laughed.

Yes, while dad explained what we were doing there, he tipped his stupid, arrogant head back and guffawed like it was the funniest thing he'd ever heard.

Then he looked me up and down and, curling his

annoyingly attractive lip, said, "what the hell am I gonna do with her, huh?"

The shame.

He looked like a classic high-school jock, while I know I'm nothing special. Short, dumpy. A plain Jane. But still.

It hurt.

"She's just come of age," my dad wheedled.

My head snapped to him. "Dad, don't even!" I yelled, with the last scrap of dignity I had.

Was he really trying to use my virginity as a bargaining tool?

Maybe I imagined it, but I thought a flicker of interest lit in arrogant dickhead's eyes. "I have to marry her, right?"

Dad dipped his head sycophantically. "That's part of the deal."

"Not interested," he snarled, turning on his heel and leaving us standing there.

It was a long drive back home.

"Can't believe you embarrassed me like that, Scout," dad kept muttering. "That was your one chance, and you sure blew it."

"*I* blew it?" Finally, I snapped. "Dad, I might be living this weird stone-age life with you, out in the ass-end of nowhere, but that doesn't mean you can treat me like I'm your property!"

He slammed the brakes on so hard, my face almost hit the glovebox.

"What do you think's gonna happen when the *Final Fiasco* comes, Scout? You think it's all gonna be gender equality and feminist marches? Nope. Only the strong will survive. And that sure as hell won't be you. Won't be any women."

I stared at my dad as realization seeped into my poor brain. This is what it was all about. It was never about survival. It was about recreating a backward society where men ruled over women.

"Your mom sure did a number on you, didn't she?" I said quietly.

For as long as I can remember, I've been hearing about dad's screwed up childhood. How his mom favored his elder brother and treated dad like crap. Well, here's dad's revenge.

Except there's no way that I'm gonna be the target of it.

"Watch your mouth, young lady," he growled.

I shuffled down in my seat. I was done speaking anyway, because an idea was beginning to spark in my mind. And for the rest of the journey, I let it grow.

As the truck finally pulled up in front of the dump I've learned to call home, I told him:

"I want to compete in the succession trial too, dad."

* * *

FAST FORWARD SIX days and here I am in the back of the truck again. Blindfolded, this time, with my older brothers on either side of me.

Prior to coming up with the idea of selling me off, dad had been muttering about choosing one of his sons as his successor, "should anything happen to him." His plan was to put them through a survivalist challenge. Whichever one made it home first would win the crown. And I've decided I want to be a part of it, too.

Once dad stopped laughing his ass off, he agreed readily.

Which makes me think he's actually keen to be rid of me, then he won't have to deal with the shame of me being a reject. He's probably hoping I'll get eaten by a bear.

Me, I reckon I've got a chance of winning. My brothers might be twice the size of me, and a whole lot better at chopping wood, but I'm the one who's done most of the foraging and trapping so far. I know how to use the sun's position for direction, read the signs written in the undergrowth, and follow animal trails without leaving a trace.

And if I don't win?

Well, anything's got to be better than waiting around until dad decides to make me the target of his next stupid plan.

Of course, my brothers—who are assholes, by the way—are determined to make things as difficult for me as possible. They've been calling me names and pinching and jabbing me throughout the journey. Showing off about how tough and fearless they are.

Methinks my brothers doth protest too much, and I told them so, but like anything else that's come out of a book, it went right over their thick heads.

We've been driving for a real long time, but at last dad pulls over beside a nondescript clump of trees.

"Get out," he barks.

I yank off my blindfold in time to catch Owen with his blindfold a little raised. He's been cheating. Of course, he has.

My brothers jump out and immediately start peeing in the bushes.

"Scout?"

I turn to my dad.

He hands me a small white plastic device. "Keep that with you."

"What is it?"

"It's a GPS tracker. In case you don't make it."

I hesitate, then pocket it.

"I'll come find you. Just make sure you keep your —" He nods in the direction of my crotch. "Purity intact."

My mouth is still hanging open as he waves goodbye to my brothers. "I'll expect you back in a week, at the earliest," he calls.

And he's gone, in a cloud of dust and creaking suspension.

There's something different in my brothers' eyes as they turn back to me, zipping up in unison.

Fear.

They're both out of their depths, and they know it.

I grit my teeth, knowing they don't deserve what I'm about to say. "Need a couple of pointers?" I ask.

"From you?" Vinny lets out a bellow of laughter. Then he treats me to a long, disdainful look.

"See ya later, little sis," Owen says in that sneering way of his.

"If we see you at all," Vinny adds.

Cackling like hyenas, they start hiking down the blacktop the way we just came.

I pause and take in the afternoon sun, noting the shadows it casts from the nearby pines. Then, shouldering my backpack, I step into the forest and start walking in exactly the opposite direction.

2

Scout

*P*urity, *my ass.*

I'm heading slowly west, trying to take note of everything around me, while all the time my head is ringing with my father's words.

Of course, I'm still a virgin. I've grown up in the wilderness, rarely even laying eyes on anyone who's not a blood relation. But the thought that my dad is planning to use this as a commodity? My blood boils.

Right now, I want nothing more than to track down the biggest, gnarliest mountain man I can find, and demand he ravish me.

Happens to be one of my favorite fantasies, actually.

Sometimes, when I'm in lying on my old army cot trying to get to sleep, I imagine some feral, muscle-bound guy striding into our underground bunker, taking one look at me and insisting I'm *his*. He throws me over his shoulder and hauls me off to his cave or log cabin or whatever. Then he tells me how beautiful I am, strips me naked and teaches me *alll* about love.

I sigh. So far, my sex education has been lacking, to say the least. But I'm ready to learn.

I snatch the GPS tracker out of my pocket. There's a little green flashing light in the top-right corner, showing it's working.

I lift it up high and toss it into the trees.

There.

No one can track me out here now.

No one at all.

A spot in between my shoulder blades prickles. And if I don't manage to find my way back home?

Scout, it was never your home.

You're free now.

You can be anyone, do anything.

I repeat that thought over and over as I plunge through the deep undergrowth.

I'm free.

I can start over. I never have to see my crazy family again.

I can find my way out of the forest and look for the nearest small town. See if it's a place I might want to live. I don't have any money, of course, but I can probably barter some of the stuff in my backpack. Maybe the folding bow my dad was so proud of getting for each of us.

I keep walking, dreaming of living in a modern apartment. One with a queen bed and closet. A vanity filled with make-up and perfume. A whole collection of hairbrushes.

But as the sun drops lower in the sky, reality hits:

I'm deep in the wilderness, about to spend my first night without a roof over my head.

I've got a sleeping bag and a hammock, and that's all. Nothing to ward off the beasts that prowl around in the darkness. Least of all the bears.

Oh, god. The less I think about the bears, the better.

It's almost dark now and I should set up camp. All I need is two solid tree trunks around eight feet apart, and a little spot of bare earth beside them. I pass a few okay options, but I keep plunging on. I'm scared to stop. Scared to pick a spot that turns out to be a big mistake.

Gradually, I realize that I really can't see anything. Trees and sky are just different grades of gray, and I keep tripping on the undergrowth.

Come on, Scout. This is dumb.

I stop, haul off my backpack and root through it until I find my wind-up torch.

Its beam is weak, but it was all dad allowed us to bring. *You think there'll be batteries in the Final Fiasco, huh?*

Staring into the darkness, I crank the handle furiously.

And that's when I see it:

A bright light in the distance.

Way brighter than a firefly, or any other natural phenomenon.

Huh, that's weird.

Maybe I'm closer to civilization than I thought.

My heart gives a little jump, and I start walking toward it.

It's rectangular, like the window of a home.

It *is* a home.

But I'm still deep in the forest. Tall trees surround the house on all sides.

I stop dead, the hairs on my forearms prickling.

An isolated house in the middle of the forest. Not a cabin or shelter, but something large and solid-looking. Kinda like a prepper's home.

There's probably somebody watching me with binoculars right now.

This is the last thing I can deal with.

Shoulders slumping, I turn away and retrace my steps.

I'll just head back a half-mile or so and find some-place to hunker down for the night. It'll be easier now with torchlight—

Dinner.

A small silver thing dashes across my path, and my reflexes go on high alert. *All* those hours of training that were supposed to create muscle memory have paid off. Silently, I reach into the side pocket of my backpack and draw out my folding bow. Without looking, I open it out and click the apparatus into place. My attention is completely focused on tracking the oblivious little rabbit through the trees. I slide out an arrow and fit it into the bow.

It clicks into place reassuringly.

I draw back the string, and—

Crunch!

Branches break right ahead of me. Like something heavy just crashed through the trees. Then something even darker than the night plunges into my path.

I raise the torch I'd forgotten I had… and gasp.

A bear! A massive one. I make out huge, bristling shoulders and long white teeth.

It's going for the rabbit, too.

I should be scared. Hell, I'm petrified.

But maybe because my stomach is rumbling like crazy, I'm also mad.

That's my rabbit.

It won't even make a dent in a bear's appetite.

I swing my bow toward the bear. Is the arrow even capable of piercing a bear's thick hide? It was designed for killing small prey.

The bear lets out a sound. I swear it sounds surprised.

Then it lunges for me.

My fingers release the arrow.

Thunk.

It hits a tree, just above the bear's left ear.

The bear lets out an angry roar.

Fuuck!

I turn and run. Suddenly the prepper house doesn't look so bad after all. I sprint toward it with everything I've got.

I'm going flat out when my foot catches something.

Oh, heck.

I'm no longer running, but in suspended animation. Then flying headlong toward the forest floor….

Then everything goes black.

3

Orion

I shove my beast back inside of me, but it's too late. She's sprinting away from me at full pelt.

Feisty little human. She's barely half my height and a tenth of my weight, but there was a challenge in her eyes. She *wanted* that rabbit. And she was willing to fight for it—as that goddamn stinging at the tip of my left ear testifies.

She's quick, too, arms pumping, long blonde hair streaming out behind her...

Then her foot catches on a vine, and she goes down *hard*.

Damn, that's gotta hurt. I go after her.

She's sprawled out facedown, her bulky backpack

still on her shoulders and her blonde hair fanning out around it.

Where on earth did she come from? I couldn't have picked a more isolated spot for my home—just like the fates told me to. But somehow, this young human female has made it all the way out here. Surely, she can't have come alone. As I approach her, I inhale hard, my beast's sensitive nose separating out the rich odors of the forest.

No other humans or shifters close by. She is alone.

All alone in my territory, my beast purrs.

Ignoring it, I crouch beside her and move her hair off her neck to feel for her pulse.

Holy crap.

The feel of her skin and hair sends insane tingles through my body. I've never touched a female before— not a human one, anyway. I had no idea they would be so soft, so silky. It's like touching a piece of heaven itself. My beast lets out a deep purr of delight.

There's her pulse—strong, and a little fast. Well, of course. She just had a helluva fright.

She doesn't stir at my touch. She must be unconscious.

My big ol' hands are used to chopping wood, building and carving, but I force a gentleness out of them that I never knew I had. I slip her backpack off her shoulders and slide the straps down her slender arms. Then I straighten her right arm and carefully roll her onto her back.

My head spins and the heavens come crashing down.

She's beautiful. The most beautiful thing I've ever seen.

Her eyes are closed; thick, dark eyelashes resting on her cheeks, while her lips are a little parted. Damn, they're lush. So pink and glossy. I have to stop myself from dipping my head and pressing them with my own feral ones. Her skin is tanned and covered in freckles, and it glows with youthful radiance. Her hair, a cascade of gold strands, falls back from her forehead like a halo.

Time seems to stand still.

Because something powerful is taking hold of me. My heart is storming, its thunderous beats reverberating through my chest like war drums. Shivers vibrate through my limbs, and each breath I take feels like a tempest pouring in and out of me.

She's *The One*.

The one I'm supposed to be with. The one the fates set out in the stars above.

Mine, my beast roars. *Mine. Mine. Mine.* A claim as primal and undeniable as the pounding of my own heart.

I've been waiting for her for so long. Hoping, wondering. Dreaming.

But I hadn't expected her to be unconscious when we first met.

Time rushes forward again.

She's injured and in need of my help.

I hunker down and ease one arm around the back of her neck, and the other beneath her knees. Her clothes —a loose khaki button-down and shorts which leave her long legs bare—look kind of masculine and are way too big for her. But when the tender backs of her knees press against my forearm, my heart soars into the tree-tops and beyond.

Carefully, I straighten up. I don't want her to awaken until I've gotten her safely indoors. She's as light as a feather in my arms. As I walk, I scan her anxiously for injuries. There's nothing on her face to indicate she hit her head. Hopefully she just fainted from the shock of failing to take out a grizzly. Both her knees are scraped though. I'll need to tend to them. The best thing would be to let my beast lick them clean, but she'll need time to understand that her mate is half-man, half-bear.

With every step, my heart pounds a crazy tattoo of yearning. Every breath I take is filled with the scent of her, driving me to the brink of madness.

I'm taking my girl back to my lair.

My beast's fur burns my skin. It can hardly contain itself. All it wants is to claim her, right now.

My front door slides open automatically, then closes silently behind me. I carry my girl through to the ground-floor living room and lay her out gently on my sofa.

The room is dimly lit, and the glow from my tropical fish tank is soft blue. On the floor below, which is visible from the edge of the mezzanine, my saltwater swimming pool glitters invitingly. I can't wait for her to see it all. I sure hope she likes it.

She gives a little groan, and I crouch down at her side so my massive bulk doesn't scare her.

Every bit of me is as tense as that bow she shot me with. Every nerve of my body is waiting on her, desperate to see her reaction when she opens her eyes and glimpses her mate for the first time.

Will she feel the way I did?

Will she know me in that first second?

Her eyelids flutter and I hold my breath. I won't breathe again until I see what color her irises are.

Slowly, slowly, the thick fringes of her eyelashes part and two orbs, the shade of spring moss, glitter like jewels.

A sigh of delight rushes out of me. I just knew my mate would have green eyes, and they're even more beautiful than I could've imagined.

But her pupils are contracting to pinpricks, and she gives a shriek of fear.

"Hey, it's okay," I tell her, then cringe at the sound of my voice. It's kinda gruff and scratchy, because I haven't spoken in who knows how long.

"You were hurt. You were running from a bear and you fell and passed out."

Frowning, she tries to lift herself up on her elbows.

"Hey, take it easy. You might've hit your head."

She lifts her hands and feels her head and face all over. "Don't think so. I mean, nothing hurts."

My bear purrs.

The sound of her voice. It's like honey converted into soundwaves. Or tinkling streams. Shit, I'm not good with this kind of stuff. All I know is that it's the sweetest sound I've heard in my life. I can't wait to hear her say my name. Hell, call it out in ecstasy while I'm deep inside her and her nails are tearing up my back.

"My knees hurt though," she mutters, craning her neck to get a better look.

"They're a little grazed, but I've got a first aid kit," I say quickly. I'm suddenly aware that I'm naked, and that humans aren't really cool with that.

She lets out a groan of acknowledgment and lets her head fall back against the sofa cushion. She's exhausted. I see it in her pallor of her skin, the dark shadows beneath her eyes. What has this poor girl been through that's brought her to this wild place? When she trusts me a little, I'll get it out of her. And if I find out someone's hurt her, I'll make them wish they'd never been born.

"Been a long day, huh?"

"Yeah." Emotions shift across her eyes. "How did I wind up here?"

"I carried you."

"While I was unconscious?"

I shrug. "Yup. I lifted you off the forest floor and brought you inside."

Her eyes narrow as she takes in my modern home. She's probably thinking it seems out of place in the wilderness.

"Are you a prepper?" she asks.

"A what?"

A slow smile spreads across her face. "Doesn't matter. Are you a mountain man?"

I shrug. "Guess you could call me that."

Her smile gets even wider.

"What's funny?"

"Oh, doesn't matter." She shoves herself upright. "Are you naked?"

"Yeah. I… I was about to go swim when my security system alerted me to some movement outside and I went to investigate."

It sounds plausible enough. This house looks like it has a security system. In reality, an Alpha beast like me doesn't need one, but I can't tell her everything at once.

The most important thing is that she knows she's safe here.

Her gaze drifts over my shoulders and chest and down to my abs.

Damn. Is she trying to see my cock? It twitches, already at half-mast.

"You could've done all kinds of things to me while I was unconscious," she murmurs.

"I would never do that!" It comes out louder than I intended, and alarm crosses her beautiful face.

"You want me to touch you, you'd have to prove it to me," I say quickly.

She bites her lip. And suddenly, I'm powerless to do anything other than stare. At the flush of redness it brings. At the pearly whiteness of her teeth. My ears register the fast sound of her breathing.

"How?"

"How what?" I repeat, scarcely able to believe my ears.

"How could I prove it to you?"

She's looking at me intently, like she really wants to know. Desire pours through me like hot lava. How could my mate show me that she's ready for me to take her?

I swallow hard, willing my cock not to get any more swollen than it already is. "You'd have to kiss me," I grit out.

"Uh huh." Her eyes drift to my lips, and she stares at them for a long, long time. Then the tip of her tongue darts out and chases across her own, lovely lips. They glisten. So ripe, so ready to be kissed.

I'm dead. Totally helpless under the power of her beauty. I lean in.

"What else?" she whispers, her lips pouting so provocatively.

My dick is fit to explode. "You'd have to strip," I say automatically, since all I can think about is how this luscious body of hers is gonna look naked.

"Strip?" she breathes. And glory of glories, she shuffles closer, her hand rising to the top button of her shirt —"Agh!" she cries out.

"What is it?" My eyes dart everywhere.

"Oh, my knee."

Shit, it's bleeding again. It's worse than I realized.

Damn. How could I have let her suffer this long?

Stupid, stupid, I scold myself as I leap up. "I'll go get my first aid kit," I announce, exiting the room.

My cock is still hard, I discover as I stride along the corridor to the bathroom. It's jutting out like a flagpole.

She must've gotten a good view of it when I stood up.

Well, too late to worry about that now.

4

Scout

I must be in heaven. Out of all possible explanations for how I went from being chased by a giant grizzly bear to sitting in a luxurious home, being tended to by the hottest guy in the universe, this seems as good as any.

Well, if this is the afterlife, it seems pretty great so far. I might as well lie back on this comfy sofa and enjoy it.

This room is *unbelievable*. It's like something out of the movies. Not that I've seen movies for a long, long time. And it has *fish*. A giant tropical tank fills an entire wall. I freaking love fish. I spot a bunch of brightly-colored species that I recognize, and a whole lot more that I don't. The tank is set up real prettily with beautiful aquatic plants and little rocks and houses for the fish to hide in.

The rest of the room is so elegant, but inviting at the same time—exactly how I'd design my dream house. The complete opposite of my dad's shabby chaos.

Apart from the huge sectional sofa that I'm currently sprawling on, there are two armchairs, all done out in a velvety gray fabric. There's an antique coffee table, a fluffy cream area rug, and a whole row of bookshelves fills the wall behind me.

Directly opposite the sofa is a picture window that looks out onto the dark forest. This is when I realize that I'm on a mezzanine level, and that the window actually continues down to a lower level. And if I'm not mistaken, there's a tinkling sound of water coming from there. If only my knee wasn't busted, I'd go take a look. I'm a sucker for any kind of water feature.

Instead, I lie back against the plush sofa cushions, lulled by the aquarium's soft blue glow. I stare dazedly at the fish as they meander around doing their fishy thing, and wait for my mysterious naked man to come back.

Funny, I asked the universe for a rugged mountain man to come along and ravish me, and here he is. But he's way hotter than I imagined, and he's *ready* for me.

And when I say ready… I'd never seen a man's cock until today, but I know what it means when it's sticking up like that—it wants inside of me. I was trying not to stare at it, but it's kind of unmissable. Long and as thick as a beer-can.

My pussy clenches. I wonder what it'll feel like when it happens. If it'll hurt. If it'll even fit inside me.

Well, I'm ready to try. Any time now.

All I can think about is how much I want him to take me. That big, muscly body arching over me. Those dark eyes staring into mine. I love the way he stares at me. Like he's fixated on me or something. Like he's falling…

No. That's ridiculous. I'm probably just the only female he's seen in a long, long time, and his body can't help responding to me. I'm okay with that. He can scratch his itch, and I can ditch my purity. Quid pro quo.

A door closes in the distance, and I hear the sound of his feet striding along the passageway. My heart gives a little jump.

Here he is. All six-foot-four of him. All wild dark hair; sexy scrubby beard, and those amazing, chiseled cheekbones.

But now he's wearing jeans.

My heart sinks a little.

His glorious, musclebound torso is still bare, thank goodness, but his cock is now caged behind faded blue denim.

"You didn't have to get dressed on my account," I blurt out.

Sheesh. What the hell is wrong with me? I never thought I'd talk to a man like that. I'm not that kind of girl, at all.

He mutters what sounds a lot like, "Trust me, I did," and something flares in his eyes. Something hot and feral. When they lock onto mine, I feel… caught.

Suddenly, I know what a prey animal feels like when it's fixed in the sights of a predator. A shiver runs right through me. A long, delicious one that ends in a little tingle between my thighs.

He strides over to me, brandishing a bunch of medical supplies. I drink in his magnificent physique, the way his muscles ripple as he moves. Looking at him makes my eyeballs happy.

He kneels beside me.

"Am I alive?" I murmur.

"What?" Those laser-beam irises fix onto mine.

"Oh, just wondered if I was still unconscious, or something."

A smile tugs at his lips. "You're very much alive, trust me." There's a little drag in his voice. A growl of yearning. Fuck, that's *so* sexy.

Then he turns his attention to my injuries and his thick eyebrows furrow.

"Shouldn't have let that happen," he snarls, like he's mad at himself.

"Oh, your ear's bleeding." He shoved his hair back from his face and now I can see that the tip is torn.

"It's nothing." He dumps some liquid on a cotton swab and presses it against my knee.

"Yeeoww!" I yelp.

He sucks in air, his breath ragged. "I'm sorry, honey. This is the last time I'll hurt you. Ever."

My breath catches. I'm not used to gentleness. And I'm sure not used to being called honey. I'm used to the brutalities of prepper life. I'm used to being called a wuss because I can't chop wood as fast as my brothers.

But this mountain man, in the past few minutes has shown me more kindness than I've had in my whole life.

And those eyes are on mine again. Two huge, dark coals, surrounded by thick lashes and topped by a pair of heavy, slanting eyebrows. He's so darn handsome it's hard to look at him up close.

"I'm brave, really," I tell him.

"You've been brave long enough." He strokes my cheek with a callused fingertip. Darn, that feels good.

"How do you know?" I murmur.

"Just a feeling I get about you. A look in your eyes."

I swallow hard. "What kind of look?"

Instead of answering, he traces a line from my cheek, to my jaw, then he lifts his hand and strokes my hair. Every little touch draws trails of stardust with it. I bite back a moan.

"Who did this to you?"

I blink. "I-I fell. You know that?"

He shakes his head slowly. "I don't mean that. I mean, who's been starving your heart all these years?"

My mouth opens and closes again. I hadn't realized that's how I felt. But now he's saying it aloud, I know it's true. I've been feeling hungry for love and care for so long.

But if I talk about it now, all the defenses I've built up might start to crumble.

"I don't even know your name," I say instead.

There's a flicker of mischief in his ebony irises, like he knows what I'm doing. "Orion," he says.

"Orion." I repeat it, drawing it deep inside me. "I've never heard that name before."

"It's the name for the hunter constellation. My mom has always been interested in the stars."

From the softness in his expression, I sense he has a kind mom, and that gives me a warm feeling.

"It's Scout," I say.

"Scout." He smiles like I've handed him something precious.

I shrug. "Never been a big fan of it. Guess my dad was a fan of practical names. Everything's gotta be useful in his world."

"It's perfect," he replies. "A scout and a hunter." He continues. "Meant to be."

I stare at him, trying to grasp what he's saying. I mean, I understand his words, but they seem too huge for two people who've just met.

"Okay, done."

I look down. Somehow, he's also cleaned up both my knees, without me even noticing. "How did you do that?"

"Do what?"

"It didn't hurt."

"Good," he says, like he's not surprised. I watch while he carefully puts a band-aid on each knee.

He leans back and admires his handiwork.

"Thank you so much," I say.

"You're very welcome. Now, you must be hungry."

"Yeah, that rabbit was gonna be my dinner." I laugh. "But the bear beat me to it."

"I'm sure sorry about that."

"Wasn't *your* fault I got faced down by an apex predator."

He inhales slowly, his massive chest rising. "I felt bad for you though."

I frown. "You saw the whole thing happen?" My gaze drifts to the vast picture window. I wonder how far into the forest the view extends.

Then I remember my backpack. Everything I need for survival is in there. "I need to go get my backpack."

"I saw it. Don't worry, it's safe."

I push myself up to the edge of the sofa. "There's some jerky in there though. If the bear gets hold of it, it'll shred the whole thing."

"Scout, you're not going anywhere tonight."

I reel back. That's kinda bossy. And… uh… *sexy.*

His eyes are burning into mine again. "I'm taking care of you. This is all my territory."

"B-but the bear—"

"No one touches my property," he growls.

Property? A flood of heat goes through me. Why do I get the feeling he's including me in that?

"Okay," I manage to say, acting like my pussy isn't throbbing right now.

He gives himself a shake. "I'll get dinner started, and while it's cooking, I'll go out and grab your pack."

"That would be amazing. Thank you, again."

"You don't need to thank me. That's the least I'd do for you, Scout."

I blink at him, unsure what to say. Maybe I could just kiss him instead? My gaze flickers to those full lips again.

He straightens up. "You relax and I'll go whip something up in the kitchen."

"Oh, can I come?" I say, not wanting to be separated from him. "Maybe I can chop veg or something?"

He grins. "You can come, but you're not doing anything."

I start to haul myself up into a standing position, but he's right there, reaching for me.

"Here."

When I slide my hands into his, something incredible happens. There's this intense tingling sensation inside me. I feel like he's drawing me into him. Like our souls are connecting. Like part of me has been missing all my life, and he's finally here.

"Whoa," I mutter as he helps me straighten up.

"Guess your knees are feeling stiff, huh?"

My knees are the last thing on my mind right now, but I nod.

"Need any help walking down the corridor?"

I go still. If I say yes, will he sweep me up in his massive arms again?

5

Orion

*E*very single fiber of my being is attuned to Scout as I follow her tiny figure through the house I've built for her.

For a beautiful moment, I thought she was going to accept my help, and I was going to have her tender body in my arms again, but then she strode off. Guess her stomach was rumbling too bad for her to wait a second longer. I can hear it; it's like she's got a tiny grizzly in there.

Soon, my beast growls. *Soon she'll carry your young in her belly.*

I shush it up, and instead, my eyes feast on her long, golden hair spilling down her back and her lovely bare legs emerging from her boyish shorts. I wish I could see more of the luscious curves that I know are concealed beneath her clothes.

When she reaches the junction in the corridor, she looks over her shoulder uncertainly. She's so goddamn adorable, it takes all my self-control not to throw my arms around her.

My head spins. I'm already falling for her. Everything's happening so fast, but it's all so right. It's what I've been preparing for my whole life. All those lonely years where I never lost hope. I always knew my mate would come at last. And here she is. Even more incredible than I imagined.

"Bedrooms that way," I tell her. My beast's fur burns my skin. All it wants is to drag her off to the bedroom and mate her, right now.

I want that, too. I can't wait to strip her bare, give her my mark and make her mine forever. But first I want to know every last thing about her. I need to claim her body, mind and soul—all at the same time.

And she needs to learn that the bear she already met is a part of me. That it will cherish and protect her with its last breath.

"Kitchen that way."

I hold my breath as she enters my huge, state-of-the-art kitchen. There's every possible type of appliance and convenience, all designed in the latest fashion.

"Whoa, a chef could run a restaurant out of here," she breathes, wandering around the island, running her fingertips over the granite countertops.

"This is so cool," she says of the hanging pot racks.

"This color scheme is awesome." She takes in the peppermint green and copper accents.

With every compliment, my beast purrs. It's all for her. The fates guided me to build her the best kitchen money could buy, because I knew my mate would love to cook. I even taught myself to cook, in case I misinterpreted the signals I was receiving, and she'd prefer me to cook for her.

A couple of years ago, I was getting real down about the fact I hadn't met my mate yet. I was doing all kinds of crazy shit. Picking fights with other clans, arguing about territory, et cetera.

One day, my mom sat me down and told me to look deep inside myself and imagine my mate. She's real connected with the mysteries of the universe, and, like all bears, she believes that we all have one true mate, and we need to spend our lives looking for her.

It took me a while to connect with my inner self, but one day, it came to me: I needed to leave my clan territory and find a spot deep in the wilderness, and build a beautiful house, fit for a queen.

Everyone thought I was crazy. Our clan lives in log cabins, close together. We're in and out of each other's houses all the time, like one big, rowdy family. No one could understand why I'd choose to live alone. And I couldn't explain it either. I just knew that was real important that I was here every day, waiting for my mate to arrive.

I also knew the house had to have every possible luxury and convenience.

Luckily, I've got a ton of money stored in a vault in

my mom's house. When I was still in my teens, I invented an off-grid communication device that works through long-range radio technology. I started my own company selling it wholesale, and it took off, big time.

Still, I had no idea what luxury entailed, so I bought a bunch of those interior design magazines that humans love, and I hired some people to enact my vision.

The fates told me that water would be real important, so I had a saltwater swimming pool installed, and I added a giant fish tank in the living room.

I turned one of the bedrooms into a games room. I also hired a style consultant to fill the huge walk-in closet with beautiful human clothes and shoes and toiletries.

Then I waited, three long years, for my mate to arrive. My beast might be a hunter, but you can't rush these things—my mom warned me about that. Fate is ready when it's ready. And if you try to hurry it, you might lose out, and you'll be one of those broken shifters that never find their mate.

Today, at long last, it happened. Charging into my path, blonde hair streaming out behind her, was my mate—armed with a bow and arrow. Of course, she was supposed to shoot me. It couldn't have happened any other way. The hunter shot by his own mate. My mom's gonna be so tickled when she hears about this.

"This is so neat!" Scout is moving her hand back and forth in front of the sensor that controls the flow of water from the faucet. My chest warms. I'm dying to show her all the other cool features, but first I've gotta cook for her.

I slide out a stool from the island. "Take a seat," I tell her. "And tell me what you like to eat."

She wriggles up onto the high seat and scrunches up her nose adorably. "Anything, really."

"You'll have to do better that that." I point to my walk-in refrigerator. "There's a ton of food in there." Every week I prepare new dishes, trying to improve my skills. So far, my clan have been the grateful recipients.

She bites her lip again. It's a nervous tic of hers. When she's mine, she'll never have any reason to be nervous again. "Maybe not squirrel or rabbit. Or baked beans. Or tinned ravioli. But if that's all you have, that's good, too," she finishes in a rush.

My heart aches. This poor girl has lived with so little. What kind of people has she come from, who've failed to take care of her?

I open the fridge and stick my head inside. "How about venison steak with wild berry sauce? Or smoked sausage and potato casserole?" When she doesn't say anything, I continue. "Or wild game chili? Herb-roasted wild turkey?"

Only silence greets me. I pull my head out of the fridge. Tears are pooling in her eyes.

"Oh, little one." I rush over. "What is it?"

She scrubs at her eyes fiercely. "It's nothing."

I stand directly in front of her. "Look at me," I command.

Slowly, she raises those emerald eyes to me, the whites stained pink.

"You don't need to hide your feelings from me, Scout. I want you to share everything with me. Always."

Her eyes widen and her lips form a pretty little *O*. I probably sound real intense right now, but it's the truth, and it's better that she hears it early on.

"I-I'm just not used to nice things, I guess," she says in a small voice.

I close my eyes for a beat as the weight of fate overwhelms me. *This* was why I was supposed to build this place. To give this princess everything she's been denied so far.

"You're gonna have nice things every day of your life from now on," I tell her.

She blinks fast. Maybe I'm scaring her a little. She needs time to get used to me, to understand just how much I'm going to protect and care for her.

"How about I warm up the wild game chili?"

She nods gratefully.

"Want a soda while you're waiting? A beer?"

"Uh, a soda." She swallows hard. "You have Sprite?"

I fight back a grin. "Sure do." I grab a can from the fridge, pour it in a tall glass and add a glass straw and a squeeze of lime.

When I hand it to her, she holds it reverently in both hands. Then, I watch, mesmerized as she purses her sweet cherry lips and lowers them to the straw.

Her eyelids grow heavy, and she gives a long, drawn-out sigh, full of longing and bliss.

Damn, if she makes that sound when my cock is inside her, I'll be a happy bear.

When she opens her eyes again, I'm still staring. I can't help it. I don't even have the willpower to tear my gaze away. She's all I want to look at for the rest of my life.

"Haven't had a soda for years," she murmurs.

My beast's rough hide pushes at my skin. Something bad has happened to this girl, and as soon as she's gotten some food in her stomach, I'm gonna find out what it is. Then I'm gonna destroy everyone responsible for it.

6

Scout

Orion sets two places on either side of the island, then returns to stirring the chili. I've already asked a bunch of times if I can help, but he says my job is to sit and relax and let my knees rest up.

So, all I can do is stare at him in awe. He's a big growly mountain man and he *cooks*. Real food, with a bunch of ingredients, which smell incredible when they're mixed together. The sight of him, half-naked, stirring that big shiny pot is something I know I'll never forget.

Who is this man who lives deep in the wilderness, with this unbelievably well-stocked kitchen?

I savor the final drops of my soda, trying not to slurp with the straw. It's the first one I've had since elementary school, and every sip was pure magic.

"Want another?"

"Huh?" I'd been fixating on his buns flexing beneath his jeans, and when he turns, I'm slow to lift my gaze. In fact, I seem to be staring at his cock. Again.

He tips his head to the side, lips curling at the edges. "Another soda?"

"Oh, no, I'm good," I say, even though I feel like I could drink a whole store full of them.

His face goes stern. "Scout."

And just like that, I want to obey him. Not because I'm scared of him, but because I sense he knows exactly what I need.

"Could I please have a cola?" I say in a quiet voice.

His smile turns into a grin, and in another moment, the cola is in front of me, dark and sinful and delicious.

He brings over the steaming pan of chili and ladles out two big bowlfuls. Then he sits down opposite, positioning himself carefully so he doesn't bump against my grazed knees. Having him so close is doing all kinds of things to my body. I feel tingly and kinda overwhelmed, like part of me wants to go hide in the bathroom, but the other part just wants more and more.

"Thank you, so much," I say.

"Don't thank me till you've tasted it," he says and digs in.

I blow on a forkful, put it in my mouth, and my tastebuds *explode*. "Wow," I murmur. It's all I can say as I eat one dreamy mouthful after another.

I sense Orion's eyes on me the whole time. "Not too spicy?" he asks. "Enough salt?"

"It's just perfect," I assure him.

When I'm halfway through the plate, I slow down. He must think I eat like a beast. "I'm sorry. I guess I've been hungry for a long time."

His thick dark eyebrows tug together. "You don't just mean today, do you?"

I get a clutching feeling in my chest, and I shake my head. The truth is, I'm always hungry. There's never enough food at home. Our crops don't grow so well in the land dad picked out for us. All we eat is meat and gnarly potatoes.

Anger flashes across Orion's handsome features. He pushes his empty plate aside and fixes me with a serious look.

"Now, are you gonna tell me what you were doing out here, all alone in the wilderness?"

My breath catches. My family has always been all about secrets. Not sharing information with outsiders. People who might want to destroy *our way of life*.

But Orion's dark eyes are gazing into mine like he's not gonna quit until I tell him. In the past couple of hours this stranger has shown me more care and respect than my parents have shown me my whole life.

"I'm on a mission," I tell him.

"A mission," he echoes, looking at me in that fixated way of his.

And I tell him everything.

Well, most of it.

How my dad's gotten crazier and crazier over the years, and my mom's not strong enough to protect us. How he took me out of school and made us move to the forest and live this pitiful lifestyle, while we all wait for the *Final Fiasco*.

I'm so embarrassed for Orion to hear these things about me. I know from long experience how mad it all sounds. The kids at school seemed repulsed by my weirdness, and now I worry he will be, too.

The only thing I haven't mentioned is that dad is planning to broker my virginity. That's one humiliation I'm not willing to share.

When I'm finally done, my cheeks are burning and I can't look at him.

A long silence rings out.

All those mean words flood into my mind:

Weirdo. Freak. Loser.

I can't stand for him to see me that way.

I wanted him to take my virginity, but now it's much more than that: I'm starting to care about him. And the thought of him rejecting me is like a punch in the guts.

"I've gotta go to the bathroom," I mumble, jumping down from the stool.

But I've forgotten about my knees, how stiff the band aids have made them, and I stumble. A silly little cry escapes my lips and I brace myself to hit the deck.

Quickly—quicker than humanly possible—Orion is right there, catching me up in his huge arms.

"Steady, little one," he says in his deep growly voice. "You hurt yourself?" His eyes are so full of kindness, I almost tear up again.

Sheesh, I swear I haven't cried in ten years. You can probably imagine the kinds of things my dad says about weak little crybabies. They're the first ones who'll be devoured in the *Final Fiasco*, in case you're wondering.

"No," I mumble. "I'm good. Just over-tired."

"You poor thing," he says in a low voice. "How could they have abandoned you like this? You should've been treated like a queen. A precious jewel."

I stop breathing. "That's not how my family sees me," I choke out at last.

A muscle in his jaw flexes. "That's their loss," he mutters. "But I promise you, you'll never be abandoned again."

He pulls me closer and I go with it, relaxing against his big, naked body. When I close my eyes, something sweeps through me. A feeling of something opening that's been closed tight for too long. I want to wrap my arms around his waist and nuzzle my face against his pecs.

"It's been a long day, hasn't it?"

"Mmm…" I say.

"Let me show you where the bathroom is."

Is it silly that I'm disappointed when he releases me?

He guides me along the hallway to the bathroom, then closes the door softly behind me.

The bathroom is as high spec as the rest of the rest of the house, all luxurious and sparkling. I swear my family's entire bunker could fit inside it. Heck, if they moved in here permanently, it would be a gigantic life upgrade. Everything is just so *nice*, from the stack of fluffy white towels beside the sink, to the delicious smelling soaps—

Whoa…

I freeze in front of the softly lit mirror above the sink.

I haven't really seen my reflection in years.

Before dad dragged me off like a sacrificial cow to be rejected by my suitor, I peered at myself in the only mirror that my family owns—a filthy, cracked hand mirror. But I couldn't see a whole lot in the speckled surface.

I've grown up. The puppy fat has gone from my cheeks, and my eyes seem less rounded, while my lips have gotten fuller. An adult woman stares back at me.

A woman who looks like she's been sleeping in a bush. My hair is all matted, and there are smears of dirt on my face.

Oh man, I probably smell bad, too. Not something I've had to worry about in a long time, since no one showers a ton in the prepper world. But here, in this beautiful house, with this man who smells incredible...

Yes... he smells like fresh pine forests and spring air just after a rainfall, mingled with something spicy and primal. I only just realized, but I've been smelling him subconsciously all this time.

Whereas I probably smell like sweat and dirt and animal pelts.

God, this is embarrassing.

I wash up as best I can, then I slip out of the bathroom. I'll just go do the dishes, then I'll ask if it's okay if I take a shower.

But when I get back to the kitchen, Orion's not there.

The dirty dishes have disappeared though. Maybe he went to relax in the living room?

I try to remember the way as I pass through the corridors of his vast house. My brain is really not working well right now. Talk about system overload.

After a couple of wrong turns, the low blue lighting glows from the living room, like it's beckoning to me. My heart lifts as I step into the lovely room. There's no sign of Orion, but a splashing, tinkling sound draws me across the cream-colored area rug to the edge of the mezzanine. I peer over the rail.

And I gasp at the sight that greets my eyes.

7

Scout

There's a large indoor pool on the lower level with a beautiful rock formation at one end. But that's not what's catching my eye.

No, the thing that's possessing my vision—heck, my entire body right now—is the gorgeous man standing in the middle of it. Orion is facing away from me, peering through the picture window at the dark forest beyond.

I hold still and drink him in. Every ridiculously gorgeous bit of him. The water comes up to his waist, but he looks like he's already been under, because his hair is dripping wet, and rivulets of water are meandering down the muscular splendor of his back. His hands are wide apart, resting on the infinity-style edge of the pool, and he looks focused. I wonder what he's thinking about. Probably wondering why he let this grubby little prepper loose in his house.

Damn, I could stare at him all night. But what if he knows I'm here? It's going to be pretty freaking weird of me to keep gawking at him and not saying anything.

I clear my throat.

He turns to face me.

The water swirls, and one of the underwater lights hits him at just the right angle, and… holy crap, he's naked again. I can just make out the long, thick shape of his cock beneath the surface.

"Hey," he says, like everything's totally normal and he didn't just catch me with my mouth hanging open.

"H-hi, I was wondering if I could take a shower," I blurt out, my cheeks warming.

He flashes that sexy smile of his. "Plenty of water right here."

I blink. "Oh… I mean, I'd better have a regular shower, to get clean and all."

"Nothing better than salt water. It's all natural." He wades over to the side of the pool and presses a button. Immediately, a waterfall starts gushing from the rockery at the far corner. "Regular shower here," he says. And in case I needed a demo, he stands right under it, tipping his head back and letting it cascade all over him.

Oh, god.

It's a sight to make a girl's clit throb out of control. The most inviting thing I've seen in my entire life.

I stand there, worrying at my lower lip.

I think about how far Orion is out of my league.

I think about being rejected by that prepper asshole. And about my dad and his obsession with my purity.

Then I think about the way Orion looks at me. Like I'm the only person who exists in the entire world.

Heart beating fast, I turn around and look for a way down to the pool. There's a spiral staircase off the side of the hallway. I follow it, treading carefully on the narrow metal steps.

Wow, I feel like I've arrived at a jungle oasis. The air is deliciously humid and there are exotic plants and vines hanging everywhere. But I only notice all this for a second before my vision lasers in on Orion.

He's stepped away from the giant rainforest shower, and he's standing, hands on hips, watching me intently.

I take a deep breath.

This is happening.

Then I unbutton my ugly shirt. I pull it off and toss it aside. I'm too embarrassed to look him in the eye, but I know he's tracking my every move. I unbuckle the too-big belt, and shove my threadbare shorts down. My underwear is an abomination, so I'm real quick tearing it off—first my bra, then my panties.

Here I am, naked in front of a man for the first time ever. Automatically, my hands rise up to cover myself.

"Scout," Orion growls.

Right away, I drop them again.

I stand, cheeks burning, pussy tingling while he scans every part of me.

"Look at me." His voice is hoarse.

I stop breathing.

Then slowly, I raise my chin.

His dark eyes are fixated on me, and the way they're glowing is almost inhuman.

A shiver runs right through me, turning my nipples into aching peaks.

"Come to me, little one."

Every word is a pulse of desire between my thighs.

As if he's gotten me hypnotized, I begin to walk toward the pool. My legs are trembling, but I force myself to keep going, keeping my hands loose at my sides.

There's a set of steps in the corner.

Don't trip, I tell myself as I walk down them slowly.

It's as warm as a bath. My pussy disappears below the surface of the water, then my belly, then my nipples. Instinctively, I start to swim.

I spread my arms and legs wide in the breaststroke. Wow, it feels so *different* being naked in the water. So liberating.

I'm overwhelmed with shyness as I approach Orion, but the desire in his eyes gives me confidence. I stop a couple of feet away. Below the surface of the water, I can make out the dark, thick outline of his cock. It's hard.

Because he wants me.

My feet feel for the bottom of the pool and I straighten up. But it's shallower here, and my breasts emerge from the water. My instinct is to duck down again, but a stronger force keeps me standing up straight, feeling the heat of his gaze on them. My nipples are so hard they hurt. And something tells me that only his touch will ease them.

"Better than being in the shower, huh?" he says, and the tension breaks.

I grin. And I remember that I still need to get clean.

He follows my gaze to the waterfall. "There's a natural soap in the dish there. You can use it to wash up if you need to."

"Oh—" I wade over to it, locate the dish, and an olive-green bar of soap. Orion reaches over and presses a button, and the flow of water starts up again.

I lather up my hands and get to work.

And Orion watches me.

I feel like I'm in a dream. I'm naked, in front of a naked man, with a hard on, who's unashamedly watching me wash myself.

But somehow, it feels right.

The waterfall pounds all around me, stopping me from feeling so awkward as I lather up my hands and wash my upper body. Then I wash my face; then I rub the bar all over my head and wash my hair thoroughly.

Now, I need to wash my lower half, too. I can't put it off any longer. I climb up on the steps at the side of the waterfall so the water only comes up to my knees, and I wash my legs. The band aids are staying on well—they must be waterproof. I go higher and higher, then finally I slide my hand between my thighs and soap up my pussy.

A groan breaks from Orion's throat.

My head jerks up. He's staring at me harder than ever, his massive chest rising and falling.

Oh, god.

I might be a virgin. Never been kissed, never been touched.

But this is the night of my wildest dreams and I'm going to enjoy every minute of it.

Under his hot gaze, I work my hand between my legs, letting him see everything. I've never grown a lot of hair down there, and I know my pussy lips are exposed. When I spread them a little with my fingers, he lets out another groan—ragged, helpless sounding. He's such a big, strong man, but right now, he's under my power. And it feels incredible.

Hardly knowing what I'm doing, my other hand lifts up and I cup one of my breasts, tweaking the aching nipple.

I'm so wet. A sigh escapes my lips.

Shit, am I really masturbating in front of him now?

Suddenly embarrassed, I step back into the water flow and rinse off.

I hardly dare open my eyes again.

But when I do, he's taken a step closer.

"Let me kiss you," he growls.

"Please," I manage to say.

And I'm in his arms. Pressed tight against his body. Instinctively, I wrap my legs around his waist and my arms loop around his neck.

For a long time, he holds me like that, gazing deep into my eyes. Searchingly, like he's trying to understand something about me.

Then he presses his lips to mine.

Oh, they're so soft.

I swear I almost pass out.

He's real gentle at first, and it makes my heart lift how he's being so tender with me.

Then he angles his jaw and pushes my lips apart. I feel the touch of his tongue against my own, slick and velvety. He slides it in, and I open my mouth more, wanting it. Wanting all of him inside me.

I love the way he holds my head in his big hands as he kisses me deeper and deeper. Love how our bodies slide together, all wet and slippery.

His cock keeps pressing up against the cleft of my ass, before he jerks it away again like it's a beast he can barely keep under control. But all I can think is how much I want it inside me.

"Scout," he groans. "You drive me crazy."

I've never liked my name, but I love the way he says it. Full of passion and longing.

I let my body drop down a little, maneuvering so that his cock rubs against my pussy.

Whoa… an intense charge of heat rushes through me. And when I move my pussy up and down his cock, it happens again… and again. If this is how it feels on the outside, how's it gonna feel when it's inside me?

My pussy aches so bad. Somehow, I know that only Orion's cock will make it feel better.

Clinging tight to his broad back, I angle my entrance right over the end of his cock…

And gasp.

So big. No way that's going to fit inside me.

At the same moment, Orion jerks away from me. "Too soon, little one," he grits out.

His eyes are wild, feral with desire. And it's so darn sexy.

"But I want this." I hear the whine of need in my own voice, but I'm way beyond controlling it.

He touches his forehead to mine. "Tell me why, baby girl."

I hesitate. A few hours ago it was because I wanted to be wild and lose my "purity" to the first hot mountain man I could find. But now it's so much more than that.

I feel like he's the one. The one I'm supposed to be with.

But how can I tell him that? He's gonna think I'm crazy.

"Because I want you like I've never wanted anyone before," I say at last.

A deep grow spills from his lips.

"You want me to be your first?"

I stop breathing. "You know I'm a virgin?"

"Of course," he says, like it's real obvious.

"Oh." I bite my lip. Is it because he couldn't get inside me? Or something else? I'm too embarrassed to ask.

"I'm not going to rush things with you, Scout," he says. "I just want to make you feel real good."

I open my mouth to say I already feel pretty darn good, but he's walking me across the pool. I'm going backward, so I'm not sure what he has in mind until he gently deposits me on something smooth and sloping. It's like an in-pool lounger. When he lays me back on it, my back and ass stay in the warm water, while my upper parts break the surface.

Orion arches over me, his dark eyes raking me from

head to toe. Then he dips his head and takes one of my nipples in his mouth.

His mouth is hot and hungry, sucking hard, while grazing a little with his teeth. All I can do is grip his wet hair in my fists and moan. *Holy hell.* It's even better than I dreamed.

He moves onto the other one, his huge hands grasping my breasts possessively. He's so good; so skillful. He must've had a ton of lovers.

And he's driving me wild.

Hardly knowing what I'm doing, I lift up my legs and hook them around his hips, needing to feel his cock against my pussy again.

His butt muscles tense, and he starts to thrust. One, two, three times… his cock slides between my lips and shoves at my entrance—

"Scout." He draws back sharply. "I'm not gonna claim you tonight."

"Claim me?" I echo.

"Make you mine," he growls.

I go still. I thought maybe he wanted to fuck a kooky little prepper girl before sending her on her way. But *claiming* sounds like a whole lot more than that?

"It's not just sex," he says, like he read my mind.

"What is it?"

He strokes my face, his nostrils flaring as he slowly exhales. "It's everything. It's forever."

My mouth opens and closes. He's saying he might want to be with me *forever*?

How can he know that when we've only just met?

Well, I guess he knows all the worst stuff about me already.

"Tonight, I'm gonna make you come." He cups my ass and my pussy lifts up, out of the water. He stares at it intently.

"What a perfect virgin pussy," he murmurs. My legs are spread wide, and I know he can see everything, but I force myself to hold still. And the longer he looks, the wetter I get.

"It's gonna be so tight around my cock." He lowers his head and gives it a long lick.

Fuck.

"My cock is the only one it'll ever know."

Lick.

"I'm gonna stretch it out so it fits me and only me."

Lick.

"And I'm gonna claim it every single day."

Lick.

He keeps on licking me and talking to me all dirty, and I'm squirming, desperate to feel him on my clit. When he finally puts his lips around it, my hips jerk like crazy.

His tongue flicks back and forth across my swollen bud, and every so often, he plunges his tongue inside me. All I can do is tug on his hair and moan.

So good. Every little thing he does.

I start to tremble all over.

"You gonna come for me, little one?" he growls.

"Yeah?" I pant.

"That's right, come hard. Right in my face."

And I do.

He latches onto my clit again and it happens. A deep shuddering builds up in my core, and I *explode*. Waterfalls and rainbows and stars swirl through my body and mind while I orgasm under this gorgeous man's tongue. I cry and moan and thrash, and he doesn't quit. He keeps on licking me and licking me until he's wrung every drop of my orgasm out of me.

"Whoa," I mutter at last, my body going limp.

When I next open my eyes, Orion is looking at me with appreciation. "Wild woman," he says in an undertone. Then he gathers me up in his arms. "So fucking sexy, Scout." He kisses me softly, tenderly. I'm so relaxed, I'm barely aware that he's carrying me across the pool.

"I better get you to bed. You've had a long day."

8

Orion

*M*y dick can't take any more. Before I've even closed Scout's bedroom door, I grasp it in my fist. It's swollen like crazy, veins standing out all around it and precum dripping from the head.

It took everything I had not to stick it into my girl tonight. The way she kept riding it; her tight little virgin hole pushing down on it, all wet and slippery, like she was inviting me in. She's so luscious. So ripe and ready for me.

I know she's mine, of course. No other man is ever going to touch her. But before I take her, I need her to know about my beast. Get her ready for my mark.

I leave her door open a crack. She's asleep already. After she multiple-orgasmed under my tongue, she got all soft and sleepy. Not so sleepy that she didn't try to get at my dick one more time. But I knew she needed her rest. I towel-dried her hair, then I put her to bed in one of the guest rooms. I've got all kinds of nice things for her to wear, but there was no time to show her all that. Instead, she slid between the sheets buck naked.

I can't resist peeking into the room one more time. It's dark, but my beast's keen eyesight has no trouble picking out her lovely features. Her thick eyelashes closed in sleep. Those pursed cherry lips. I wonder how they'll feel around my cock. Her little jaw stretching wide to accommodate me—

Fuck.

There's a splattering sound as my cum hits the door. Hadn't even realized I'd been pumping my dick, but now my seed is spurting from the end of it like a firehose.

Should've been flooding her womb instead, my beast growls.

Soon, I tell it. *And every day after that.* Just like I told Scout while I was eating her pussy.

Well, it's best she knows what to expect from mating a horny shifter.

Still, my bear smirks at the sight of my cum dripping down her door. It's a simple beast, and like all animals, it likes to mark its territory.

9

Orion

I didn't sleep a whole lot last night. My beast was too darn excited to let me rest.

Now I've found my mate at long last, and it knows she's asleep under my roof, a jerk-off wasn't gonna be enough to satisfy it. Nope. It needed outta me. Eventually, I had to get up and head out into the wilderness for an almighty hunting session.

But as soon as I hit the forest, a bunch of unfamiliar scents assailed my nostrils. My beast was *mad*. This is *my* territory—here and for miles around. It's marked every inch of it, with its claws or its piss, and other predators know better than to invade it. But last night, the undergrowth was humming with the stink of a horde of different shifters. They've probably been tracking Scout from the moment her dad dumped her on the roadside. Can't say I blame them. Her innocent, ripe scent must have been fucking intoxicating. They were probably oblivious to anything other than claiming her.

Not. Fucking. Happening.

My beast went a little crazy, tearing up everything in its path. Warnings of what's gonna happen to anyone who thinks they can invade my space. It wouldn't quit until it'd patrolled the whole territory twice over—and caught enough meat to last for a month. Probably a good thing, because I'm darn sure that as soon as I've gotten my cock inside my girl, I won't want to go anywhere for a long, long time.

I yawn and stretch as I bound out of bed. Despite the short sleep, I feel good. Full of energy. All these years I've been preparing for Scout's arrival, and here she is at last. Even more delicious and sexy than I'd hoped. I can't wait to show her around the rest of the house, explain to her that everything here is hers.

I go to the kitchen and set about making breakfast. I wonder what she likes to eat. She seemed so grateful for everything last night. Poor thing. Sounds like she's been living on junk all of her life. From now on, I'm gonna make sure every meal is fit for a queen.

Because she is a queen. The most regal and exquisite being that ever lived.

I wind up laying out all the possible ingredients on the counter so I can see what catches her eye: eggs, bacon, milk, flour, hollandaise sauce, mayo. Spinach, mushrooms, sausages, maple syrup, wild berry jam, granola, bread—white and wholegrain—smoked salmon, muffins.

Everything is fresh or homemade; nothing comes out of a packet. Even before I knew how crazy her family is and the diet her father has been subjecting them all to, I sensed she'd want to eat healthy, wholesome food.

Every nerve in my body is on high alert, waiting for Scout to emerge from her slumber. But it's still early, I remind myself. She needs her rest.

I make a coffee with my fancy machine. I bought it for Scout. The fates were kinda vague on whether she liked coffee or not, but I didn't want to take any chances. It's the best that money can buy, and every morning I challenge myself to make a better one than the day before. Think I've got cappuccinos just about perfect now. I even sprinkle a bunch of cocoa powder on top in a pretty heart pattern. If my clanmates saw me doing that, they'd laugh their furry asses off. Believe it or not, I've always been the biggest, toughest bear in the clan. The one most likely to give up on civilized living and sleep in a cave. And then two things happened: I accidentally came up with a business idea that humans went crazy for, and the fates told me to go prepare for my mate.

Now I'm living like one of those wealthy humans. Gotta admit, it's kinda cool having all these conveniences. But they're nothing compared to the look on Scout's face when she saw the pool for the first time. My heart just about soared up through the glass roof. I knew I'd listened to the fates's instructions just right.

They told me my mate would want a beautiful, big, tropical pool where she could spend hours relaxing and swimming.

I take the coffee to the upstairs terrace to watch the dawn like I do most mornings. It's a stunning view, the sun rising over the distant mountain peaks, streaking the sky pale yellow and peach. I grin to myself. Just yesterday I was watching a fierce orange dawn, wondering if I'd ever get to share these beautiful moments with my mate, and here she is.

Down below, the forest is still hidden in darkness. A strange odor drifts back to me from last night: the sour tang of an unknown male bear. Not a grizzly. Something else big and beastly. I picked it up a couple of times, right on the borders of my territory. No prizes for guessing what it was hunting for.

My beast swells beneath my skin. Just the thought of another man touching my girl turns it mad with rage. It'll go straight for the jugular. There'll be no stopping it. I'll tear him apart. Disembowel him. Rip his gonads out and leave them for the crows to eat—

There's a sound behind me. Footsteps.

Fuck.

I probably look like a crazed lunatic right now. My skull is broadening, and I can feel my canines forcing their way out.

I take a deep breath and pull my beast back down inside me, as deep as it'll go. Then I turn in time to capture the vision of Scout padding across the bedroom that leads to the terrace. She's barefoot and wearing a towel. Nothing underneath it, my beast notes. I pick up her delicious virgin scent, unimpeded by panties.

"Hi," she says quietly. Her eyes are full of uncertainty.

Damn, did she see something of my beast? My chest aches. I never want her to feel that way about me. I want her to know she can trust me with her life.

When she steps onto the terrace, I don't hesitate; I step toward her and take her in my arms. To my delight, she lifts her chin, like a delicate flower turning toward the morning sun. Her luscious lips are pursed, anticipating the kiss I can't wait to give her.

I dip my head and kiss her.

And kiss her.

I can't let go. She's too darn irresistible. I hold her close, tangling my fingers in her silky blond hair, running my hands up and down the contours of her back. At some point I notice that her towel has come loose. Now she's delectably naked, her bare tits pressed against my chest, while my cock is doing its best to break free from my jeans.

I slip my hand between her legs. Fuck, she's wet already. I cage a growl between my teeth. When I touch her clit, she moans into my mouth. It's fucking delicious. I slide my finger a little lower and find her entrance, still barred by her hymen. Soon it'll be gone. Destroyed by my cock. Fire burns in my veins.

Claim her! my beast growls.

Could I? Lift her pretty ass up onto the terrace rail? Spread her sweet thighs, then pull out my throbbing cock and sink it into her?

The urge is taking hold of me. My beast is antsy, all riled up. The scent of her wet pussy is driving it insane.

She reaches for my zipper.

Holy shit.

I stop breathing as she slides it down—

But something moves behind her.

I freeze.

Something in the forest. Dispersing the undergrowth as it approaches.

"Wait," I whisper, shoving Scout behind me.

Shit, it's that thing.

I watch in fury as a huge, shaggy gray beast bursts through the trees. It's heading directly toward my house, flashing its yellow eyes and yellower fangs.

Fucking asshole. How can it not know this is my territory?

Because its goddamn nostrils are snuffling, scenting my girl! I can hear the repulsive sound from here.

"Oh, my god," Scout mutters.

I shoot a glance at her. She's picked up her towel and she's wrapping it around herself. That fucking prick got to see everything. He'll pay for that, ten times over.

"It's okay, baby," I tell her. "I got it. Just go inside."

"Nuh-uh." She shakes her head. "I'm staying right here."

My heart swells. She's protective of *me*. This tiny, fierce human woman. "Okay." I take a deep breath. "If anything happens, go inside and lock the doors."

Her eyes widen, but she gives a quick nod.

I turn back to the ugly, shambling beast. My first

instinct—my only instinct—is to destroy it. But it'll be a lot for Scout to deal with.

My animal huffs and snarls, but I hold it in with all my might. "You're making a big mistake!" I roar down to the monstrosity. "But I'm giving you one chance to get the hell out of my forest."

The goddamn beast gives no indication that it's heard me. Instead, it keeps approaching, until it's right in front of the boundary wall.

It stares up at me with those nasty yellow eyes, teeth bared in an insolent leer. Just when I thought it couldn't get any uglier, its human head emerges, just enough for it to speak.

"She's mine," it grunts in a voice like breaking rocks. "I'm gonna rip your throat out, then fuck her right over your dead body."

Rage pours through me like lava. "Like hell you are!" I bellow.

I don't have time to explain anything to Scout. All I can do is holler, "Get inside and lock the door," before my beast rips out of me.

I stand on the deck on all fours, foaming at the mouth and swollen with murderous rage.

A second later, I'm over the terrace rail. It's a long way down to the ground, but I crash through the trees, my claws slicing through the branches.

I hit the ground with an almighty thump and spin to face the beast.

It's as big as me—which is not something I see very often—and it stinks like hell. Like it's been sleeping in a swamp or something. Its fur is gray and matted into dreadlocks. It's the most repulsive thing I've ever seen, and it thinks it's gonna get its filthy paws on my girl?

"That virgin pussy is mine—" it snarls.

But before it can finish the sentence, I *launch*. With a primal roar, my beastly form smashes into the foul monstrosity, jaws snapping shut around its snout. A piercing screech fills the air as the beast thrashes, trying to shake me loose. But I've got it in a vise-grip, feeling its hot, reeking breath as it struggles. When it throws itself sideways, I roll with the momentum, and we crash down to the forest floor. We tumble and thrash, a whirl-wind of claws and teeth.

My muscles burn with exertion, but I refuse to relent. I slash at its face with my claws, wanting to tear its ugly words right out of its mouth. My claws are the most powerful of my clan, but it meets me, stroke for stroke, each swipe matched by a vicious counterattack. Blood sprays and the forest echoes with our bellows of rage and pain. My senses are honed to seek out its weaknesses, but it's strong. I've torn up its whole face, and it just keeps coming, shaking the blood out of its eyes.

As I lash out again and again, I think of Scout, of her beauty and toughness. Holding her image in my heart as I fight for her.

Every fiber of my being is focused on taking it out. It's a brutal opponent. My toughest ever, and I'm fighting to the death. If I don't kill it, it'll take Scout for its own. And there's no chance in hell that I can let that happen.

Suddenly, the beast pulls away from me. I go still, confused.

Then it clambers up a half-fallen tree trunk and I see what it's got in mind.

"Rooooar!" It springboards off the trunk like a fifteen-hundred-pound missile, claws aimed right at my eyes.

Not. Happening.

I duck down low and as it comes in to land, I slash with my own claws. I keep them razor sharp, and it pays off. I open up the beast's guts, using its own weight against it.

And I keep going, tearing all the way down to its balls.

The sound it makes is awful; I almost pity it.

It knocks me flat as it lands. I can take it though. I flip it over, my nostrils full of the stink of its blood and spilling guts.

Looming over it, I pull in my beast, let my human emerge.

"No one touches my girl!" I bellow in its face. With one final swipe, I tear its throat wide open. Blood gushes in hot spurts.

But I don't move until the last breath of air has left its lungs and the light has died from its eyes.

I get to my feet and turn my back on it. Ready for the vultures to pick its carcass clean.

Then I go look for my girl.

10

Scout

*M*y breath whooshes out of me.

He killed the monster. It's over.

My throat is raw from screaming, and my fingers hurt from gripping the rail so tight.

And I have no idea when the towel slipped off me —again.

All I know is that Orion turned into a bear, and fought another bear to the death.

Yup. He turned. Into. A. Bear.

One minute, this incredibly hot man was standing in front of me. And the next... he grew fur, he got a ton bigger, and his jeans turned into tiny scraps of fabric. There they are, lying in a heap on the terrace.

Then, before I had a chance to freak at the sight of a

giant grizzly right in front of me, he plunged off the balcony, headfirst.

That fight was the bloodiest, most brutal thing I've seen in my life. I was so scared for Orion. But I could see how strong he was. The other beast was as vicious as fuck, but he didn't have Orion's big heart, his courage.

So many times, I wanted to squeeze my eyes shut. But I forced myself to keep looking. I had to be brave, like Orion was being.

I hear the bedroom door open on the far side of the room. I turn around, ready to face him. I should probably pick up the towel and cover myself with it. But I don't.

There's no need to hide my body from him.

I'm his.

I know it deep in my soul.

I love him.

His footsteps pound across the dimly lit bedroom.

He's here. Stepping onto the terrace.

My heart hammers like crazy.

"Orion—" A scream bursts from my lips.

Because he's covered in blood. Just like the bear was.

His beautiful face and torso are crisscrossed with vicious wounds. I can see five-clawed slashes everywhere. Tears spring to my eyes.

"Oh, my god!" I run to him, holding my arms out, not knowing where to touch him.

He slides to a stop. "You saw all that?" There's uncertainty in his eyes. I know he's worried I'll be disgusted or something, and I can't stand it. Can't stand the thought he might feel ashamed when he's been nothing but brave.

I catch his hands and squeeze them tight. "Yes! You saved me. You're a bear-man. A-a shapeshifter?"

He gives a deep nod. "I am." Then his brow furrows. "What d'you think about that?"

I take a deep breath. There are *so* many things I'm thinking and feeling right now. I feel like I could burst from all the emotion stirred up inside me. "Turned on," I blurt out.

"Turned on?" His eyes glow, gold sparks shooting from his irises.

I nod vigorously. "You bet."

"You wanna talk about this?"

"Nope. I just want you the way you are, Orion."

With a throaty growl, he wraps his arms around me and pulls me in.

I try to be careful at first, to not hurt his poor bruised lips. But he's holding me tight and I'm losing myself in the wonder of his kiss. I forget about his injuries, forget about everything other than connecting with him. My bear-man.

Something jabs me hard in the belly. His cock, of course. Even bigger and harder than it was last night. I wrap my hand around it.

This time, he doesn't pull away. Instead, a sexy groan pours from his lips.

I tilt my head back and look him in the eye while I run my hand up and down his thick shaft.

"Fuck, Scout. You know what you're doing to me?" he hisses out.

I feel his muscles trembling, and my pussy throbs. It's so darn sexy seeing this huge bear man helpless with need.

A little smile tugs at my lips while I explore his cock, the hard ridges and thick veins bulging all over it. I cup his balls, too, feeling their weight. This is where his cum is gonna come from, I think, and my pussy spasms.

We are going to have sex very soon, and somehow this massive cock is gonna fit inside me.

When I dare raise my head and look him in the eye again, I see the fire burning in his eyes, the muscles flexing in his jaw.

I can see his bear there, too, just below the surface, and I'm glad for it. I want to know it's a part of him when he takes me for the first time.

I feel moisture between my thighs, and I press them together. I'm not just wet, I'm drenched. I'm kinda nervous, but I'm as ready as I'm ever going to be.

"Take me, Orion," I murmur. "Right now."

He runs his big hands over my shoulders, my arms, my breasts. "You're so beautiful, so perfect, Scout. And I'm all torn up."

I loop my arms around his neck. "Because you were saving me." I pull his head down and kiss him soft and deep.

His tongue slides into my mouth again. Hungry. Probing. With a helpless groan, he grasps my ass and lifts me up, perching me on the terrace rail.

It's a long way down, but I have no fear. Orion has already proved he'll protect me with his life. I wrap my legs around his waist and his cock presses against my pussy.

He slides back and forth, making me wetter and wetter. Tingles run through me.

Then he fits the head of his cock to my entrance.

Fuck, it's big.

He gives a little thrust.

Oww! I cry out in pain as his cock forces its way into me.

"Sorry, honey," he mutters.

"Don't stop." I cling on. I want this. My nails rake his back, encouraging him to go deeper. He pushes in deeper and my pussy burns as he busts through my hymen. It hurts like crazy, but I know it's gotta happen like this.

He gives a bigger thrust, and suddenly he shoves all the way inside me. All the way to the hilt.

"Ahh!" I gaze up at him, open-mouthed. I feel like he impaled me with his monster dick.

I didn't think it was possible, but somehow my pussy has accommodated him. It's pulsating around his thick shaft.

"You're mine now," he growls. "All mine."

A violent shudder runs through me. He's possessing me. Making me his.

My man. My bear. My hero.

"I'm yours, Orion. Forever."

He stares into my eyes. "I love you Scout," he rasps, stroking my cheek.

My heart somersaults. "You do?"

He shakes his head wonderingly. "Everything's

happened so fast, but I've never been surer of anything in my life. I love you, my beautiful mate."

"I love you, too." The words rush out of me. Then I give a laugh of pure happiness. It's crazy. He's covered in wounds; the body of the bear he just killed is lying in the dirt thirty feet below us, and my pussy is throbbing from the onslaught of his cock. But this is the most romantic thing I can imagine.

"And now I'm gonna make you come all over my dick," he growls, and I quit laughing.

Instead, I give myself over to the power of his cock as it pumps in and out of me.

"So darn tight," he grunts, screwing himself into me. With every stroke, the pain gets less and this amazing tingling feeling gets stronger.

"Oh, god. Orion," I mutter against his mouth. "I think I'm going to—"

I don't finish my sentence, because an orgasm rips through me. Waves of ecstasy take over my whole body, and I tip back my head and *scream* into the forest. I feel so wild, so free.

Naked, outdoors, with my bear-man screwing me senseless.

"Yeah, that's it, wild woman," Orion roars.

Suddenly, he pulls out of me. I stare at him, stunned.

"I'm gonna claim you now. But not here."

He lifts me off the rail and carries me back into the house.

11

Orion

I'm gonna make this special for Scout. She deserves satin sheets and fluffy pillows and every little soft thing her heart desires.

I carry her through to the bedroom that's all decked out in snowy white, from the walls, to the comforter, to the rugs.

Then I stop in the doorway. My dick is colored pink with the traces of her virginity. That I can definitely deal with. But the rest of it? I'm gonna get blood from all my injuries all over the white sheets, and that's not gonna be pretty for her, at all.

"Uh, better shower first," I say, turning a one-eighty.

"In the pool?" she says.

My beast pricks up its ears, detecting a hopeful note to her voice.

"You want me to claim you in the pool?" I growl.

She raises an eyebrow. "If claim means fuck me a whole lot more, that's a *hell, yes.*"

My beast purrs. Before she's finished her sentence, I'm already striding toward the spiral staircase, making for the pool like my dick's got a homing device attached to the end of it.

In a minute, I'm walking down the stone steps into the water. She gives a sigh as the warmth envelops us.

But then she gazes at me worriedly. "Doesn't it sting?"

"Huh?"

"Doesn't the saltwater hurt your wounds?"

"Shifters heal fast. Just need to get this filth off of me." I gently release her into the water, then I wade over to the waterfall and start scrubbing at my skin.

"Hey, hey." She catches my hand. "You got a wash-cloth or something?"

"Uh, over there." I point to the sink in the corner, where there's a little basket of single-use hand towels. My interior designer said chicks dig that kinda thing. I go to grab one, but Scout lays her hand on my arm.

"Let me."

I watch, awed, as she steps out of the water and retrieves a cloth. Her naked body is any man's dream, her big, round tits bouncing as she walks. And I love that she's not shy for me to see it.

She joins me under the waterfall. I try one more time to grab the cloth from her.

"Nuh-uh," she says. A stern look fills her emerald eyes, and it connects directly with my cock.

Then she washes me all over. She makes me bend down so she can reach my face and shoulders. She's washing away the marks from the beast I conquered, and preparing me to claim her.

Holy crap, that's sexy. My cock is harder than ever, sticking out like a flagpole as she works around it, gently wiping the dried blood from my hips and thighs.

At last, she stands back and examines her handi-work. "You're almost healed," she says, eyes sparkling in wonder. Christ, she looks like an angel, her hair flowing into the water and her perfect tits rising above the surface.

My beast pushes up beneath my skin, bursting with impatience. Now my cock's already been inside her, it can't understand why I've been holding back.

I reach for her with a growl.

When I flip her around, she makes a sound of surprise. But it turns into a sigh as I lift up her wet hair and plant kisses all over her neck. I grasp her lovely tits and squeeze them a little. Two perfect handfuls, with those delicious, caramel-colored nipples pebbling beneath my fingers.

I slip a hand between her thighs, feeling how wet she's getting. She's ready.

I keep my finger on her clit as I walk her across the pool. I'm heading for the in-pool lounger in the corner. I gently bend her over it, and it works even better than I dreamed. Her ass rises up out of the water; two ripe, peachy globes. I spread her cheeks, needing to see everything—her little rosebud pucker, and her perfect pink pussy, a little reddened from the intrusion of my cock.

My dick pulses. What an incredible sight.

Claim her! my beast roars.

I press the head of my cock against her entrance. She tenses at first, then I feel her relax around me, like she's welcoming me in.

Slowly, I slide my length into her. Feel her little muscles spasm around me. The sight of my dick filling her up almost makes me shoot my load.

But, no. That's not gonna happen until she's come all over my cock. Three times at least.

I pull out a little, then thrust in deeper.

She moans, and a smile tugs at my lips.

I know my baby likes that friction. So, I keep giving it to her, bit by bit.

By the time I hit home, she's all sprawled over the lounger, ass raised, begging me for more.

Every stroke is pure heaven. I hold her cheeks apart so I can watch my cock going in and out. The wonder of my monster dick filling her tiny pussy.

Her cries of pleasure are the sweetest music I've ever heard.

The rhythmic slapping of my hips pounding her ass.

The fast, ragged sound of her breathing.

I see her tiny hands gripping the sides of the lounger. "Oh, Orion. Don't stop!" she cries out.

My beast bares its teeth in delight.

No way am I gonna stop.

I pound her harder and harder, my claws biting into her hips.

She pants and moans and begs for release.

A second later, this amazing ripple travels through my cock, and she screams my name.

She's coming, all over my dick again. Her pussy spasms around me, milking my cock. And I don't stop. I keep hammering her sweet pussy while she comes over and over, calling out my name.

At last, I feel her body going slack. She's spent.

Shit, I can't hold back anymore. My canines are pushing through. I arch over her and clamp my jaws around the tender skin at the nape of her neck.

She gives a shriek of pain, but she doesn't pull away. She *knows*. My teeth are on her neck, my cock rooted deep inside of her, and I'm giving her the mark that will bond us together for life.

I hold her right where she is while I thrust harder and harder. I'm losing control of myself; My beast is taking over. It's snorting and panting, hammering itself all the way in. Faster, deeper, rougher.

"Orion!" she gasps out. Her pussy clamps around my girth one more time, and it happens—my hot cum pours out of me like a firehose, flooding her womb with my fertile seed. So fucking much of it, as if it's never gonna stop.

When I'm finally done, I wrap my arms around her, and draw her back into the water with me. I like that my cock stays inside her while she snuggles into my arms.

"You claimed me," she murmurs.

"I did." I gaze in awe at the mark on her neck. From now on, every shifter who sees it will know she's my property. She'll be able to walk through the wilderness with no fear of being attacked.

She's mine. Forever.

My beast is calm now, and there's nothing in my head but the sensation of holding my girl in my arms, her soft head pressed to my chest.

She's quiet, too. I need to check in on her.

I lift her chin with a fingertip so I can look directly into her eyes. "You okay, baby?"

The look she gives me is so serious, my chest tightens. But I'm completely unprepared for her next question:

"I shot you, didn't I?" she asks, her green eyes all narrowed with suspicion.

"What are you talking about?"

"Orion." She gets that sexy stern tone again. "That's why your ear was bleeding. It wasn't any old grizzly trying to steal my dinner. It was you!"

I shrug. "My mom always said I'd find another hunter."

Her eyes sparkle. "She did?"

I stroke her cheek. "Yup. My mom's real good with that kind of stuff."

"What else did she say?"

"That she'd also be a water sign."

She gasps. "I'm a Pisces."

"Figures." I indicate the room with a grin.

"What about you?"

"Scorpio. Most compatible signs. At least my mom says so."

"What else, what else?"

My chest warms. It's adorable how enthusiastic she is. And I've been longing to tell her everything.

"She said I needed to get ready for you, and make you real comfortable. So I built this place."

She goes still. "You built this place for *me*?"

"Yup. I used to live in a hut in my clan's territory, but I knew you needed something more. A whole lot more.

She looks around in wonder. "It's like my dream home. Everything is exactly as I'd choose it."

I laugh. "That's how I planned it."

"But how did you know what I liked?"

"The fates guided me. Along with a little help from my mom."

She gives a laugh, part disbelief, part joy.

"This is all for you, Scout."

"But… it's so much."

"My mom told me you'd be someone who'd been deprived of a lot of stuff in life."

She sighs. "Prepper life ain't easy."

There's a twinge in my chest. She's still so self-deprecating, despite everything she's been through. "I can't even imagine," I say. "But I promise you, you'll never lack anything in life again. If there's anything you need, just let me know and I'll make it happen." I raise her fingers to my lips and kiss them.

"Oh, you've done so much for me already."

"It's the least I'd do for you, Scout. Don't you understand that? You're my mate. And I'm going to spend the rest of our lives loving and protecting you as hard as I can."

She gives a little gasp. While her lips are parted, I dip my head and claim them again.

It's gonna take a lot for Scout to believe that I'm for real. I understand that.

Luckily, I've got all the time in the world. She's got my mark on her neck; my beast is sated, and all I need to do is prove to her how much I love her.

12

Scout

Orion takes my hand and leads me through his beautiful house. *My* house, as he keeps telling me.

Yesterday we barely made it out of the pool or bed, breaking only to eat, but now he's eager to show me around. It's weird though; I feel like this house has been waiting for me all this time. Like it was all complete, and the only thing missing was me.

It's all so modern, stylish and clean. I'm really not used to clean. Or modern, or stylish, for that matter.

Every room we pass through is stunning. Orion shows me how to adjust the lighting and temperature with high-tech touchpads. It's a lot to take in for a simple prepper girl; I'll probably have to ask him to show me again later.

"What about the security system?" I ask.

"It's right here." He points to himself and grins. "These ol' ears, eyes and nose are all I need. I've also marked my entire territory. The only time anyone's breached it was yesterday, when a bunch of shifters went crazy over your scent."

I blush. "T-they could all smell me?"

"Big time."

"But won't they *keep* smelling me?"

"Not now you're mated." There's a possessive growl in his voice. "Now they'll know you're mine."

My cheeks get even hotter, and so does that little spot between my thighs, which hasn't quit aching since I first laid eyes on Orion. It's embarrassing, but I also kinda like the fact that I smell different now I'm no longer a virgin. Now I'm his.

"Where are your supplies?" I ask, as he continues his tour of the house.

"Supplies?"

"In case, you know, there's a national emergency or something."

He grins. "There's a whole forest of supplies out there, trust me."

A burst of alarm goes through me. He's not taking this seriously at all. "B-but what if something poisons the forest? You'll starve."

Orion turns to face me. He gives me a long look. Then he takes my hands in his. "Scout, listen to me. The chance of that happening is very, very small. I know that's how you've been raised. But you've got to quit worrying. Now it's time to have fun and enjoy your life."

I close my eyes, and something inside me releases, like a spring that's been coiled too tight for too long. I let out a long breath. "You're right. I've been fantasizing about escaping my family for years. I don't want to live like them."

He presses his lips to my forehead. "And you won't, so long as I've got anything to do with it. C'mon, I'm gonna show you the upper level." He bounds up the stairs. His enthusiasm is infectious, and I race up after him, giggling.

There are a bunch of doors coming off the hallway. He throws open the first one.

It's a gigantic games room. There's a pool table, a foosball table, and a retro arcade machine. I wander around, my mouth hanging open. There's a giant flatscreen TV with a bunch of gaming consoles and a pile of comfy beanbags beside it; a bookcase full of board games; a dartboard, *and* a vintage pinball machine.

My heart leaps. There used to be one in the mall close to my family's old home. My bestie and I used to spend hours on it.

I think I lose a couple of minutes, pulling on the levers and muttering to myself as the ball zips around crazily.

When I next look up, Orion is watching me, eyes crinkling at the corners.

My face gets hot. "Sorry," I mutter. "Got a little carried away."

He puts his arm around me and pulls me close, planting a kiss on top of my head. "Don't ever be sorry,

Scout. "This is why I got all this stuff. To have fun with." He grabs my hand and hauls me over to the foosball table. Then he crooks his eyebrow in that sexy way of his. "You any good at this?"

I grin. "The best."

It's a good couple of hours before I'm all played out. Orion is a great opponent. He doesn't just let me win, but he encourages me a lot, and helps me with my technique.

We fall out of the room laughing and teasing each other.

"Now, I'll show you the rest of the house." Orion opens the doors to the other rooms. One is empty of furniture, but the other four are set up like luxury hotel bedrooms. They're all decorated in different styles—the one I slept in last night, all done out in pretty florals; one all white; one like a log cabin, and one in bold, contrasting colors.

"So many rooms here," I murmur.

"They'll be full of our cubs one day."

My breath catches. "We're having *cubs*?"

He embraces me from behind. "You'd better believe it," he growls. "I can't wait to fill your belly with my young."

A shiver goes through me as I absorb all these new words. "I wasn't sure if I'd ever have kids," I mutter.

He spins me around and stares at me, brow furrowed. "With these amazing genes? Why the hell not?"

I sigh. "I was worried I'd screw things up like my parents did."

"Scout…" I see his big chest rise and fall. "You're nothing like your parents."

"How can you be so sure?"

"Because you're an incredible person, and they don't deserve you."

I stop breathing, my eyes prickling.

"And I'm gonna tell you that every day, until you believe me. You're gonna be a great mom. You're so warm and caring and strong."

He presses me against his chest, and I let myself relax into him. The truth is, I want nothing more than to have Orion's cubs.

"But for now, you've gotta pick one of the rooms to be our bedroom," he says. "I decorated them differently, because I wasn't sure which you'd like best."

I wander between them like a kid in a candy store. Each one of them is the most beautiful room I've ever seen in my life. "Where do you usually sleep?"

"Guess." He plants his hands on his hips, a sexy smile tugging at his lips.

I wander back down the hallway, peering into each room. Trying to *feel* Orion, in the way he says he's been feeling me. I stop in front of the room that's decked out with wood paneling. It has a stone fireplace with a vintage leather armchair beside it, and a cozy red area rug covering the floor. A plaid comforter has been laid neatly over the gigantic bed. I imagine him sleeping there, his big, sexy body all sprawled out.

"This one, for sure."

A rumbling sound escapes his lips, and I jump.

"What was that?"

"Just my bear. It's happy that you're starting to read me."

"It's because we're mates, isn't it?"

He draws me close, stroking my hair. "It sure is. And it'll only get stronger."

I press my hand to his chest, feeling that deep, vibrating sensation that comes in time with his breathing. "I like being connected with your bear. It's a nice feeling."

"Oh, little one, this is just the beginning. One day you'll see how truly connected a bear and his mate can be."

My heart flutters. I already have his mark on my neck—it's been tingling non-stop since he gave it to me —I can't wait to see what else is in store for us.

He leads me to the floral room. "Funny, before I met you, I thought you might dig this one. That's why I set up your stuff in here."

"My stuff?"

He shows me in. On the far side of the room is a walk-in closet. I *might've* peeked in it this morning, but when I saw it was full of someone's else's possessions, I slammed the door shut again, with a mixture of guilt and jealousy.

Now he opens it. "Everything in here is yours. I wasn't sure of your size of course, so I got a few duplicates."

My mouth falls open as I take in the racks of beautiful clothes. Underneath is a row of shoeboxes. And on the shelves, I spot a bunch of expensive toiletries.

"H-how…?" I stammer.

"Just to help you settle in. Mom gave me a hand. She said you'd be traveling light, and you wouldn't have had the opportunity to pack much stuff. Go ahead, take a look."

I feel shy. But Orion keeps encouraging me, and slowly, I pull out some of the clothes and admire them. They're gorgeous and stylish, and real feminine. I stroke the soft fabrics dreamily. I've missed dressing like a girl. All these years I've been forced to wear these tomboyish clothes, and they're really not me.

"I'm just gonna go make us some coffee," Orion says, and slips out of the room. I smile at his retreating back. He's being considerate, giving me a little space.

The moment the door shuts, the final part of me that's been holding on tight lets go. I go into a trying-on frenzy, pulling one thing over my head after another.

I love everything. His mom sure has good taste. She even picked out sets of lingerie.

When Orion returns, I'm wearing a figure-hugging silver dress. It has spaghetti straps and a plunging neckline, and I'm wearing pink lace lingerie with a strapless push-up bra. I love the way it emphasizes my tits.

I hold my breath as the door swings open.

The growl that pours from Orion's throat leaves me in no doubt about his opinion.

"You have any idea how sexy you look?" Then he tilts his head to the side. "One thing missing, though." He shuffles me backwards, until my ass lands on the bed.

I watch in curiosity as he crouches down and rifles through the shoe boxes, opening one after another.

At last, he pulls out a box. "Close your eyes, baby."

I do as he says, and a moment later, something is sliding onto my bare foot, softly encasing it.

A sound of satisfaction escapes his lips.

He does the same with my other foot.

"Okay, open them."

I gasp as two pieces of silvery magnificence reveal themselves to me. The most beautiful, elegant sandals I've ever seen in my life. And they fit me perfectly.

"Christian Louboutin," he reads off the box. "My mom said these were something special."

I look from the gorgeous shoes, to my mate's handsome face and back again. He's frowning like he's worried I'm not going to like them. My heart flips.

The shoes are gorgeous, but this, *this* is what's special.

I reach for him and wrap my arms around his neck. "Thank you *so* much," I murmur. "They're the most beautiful shoes I've ever seen."

He draws back and, keeping hold of my hands, raises me to my feet. They're real high, but somehow comfortable. Guess that's the Louboutin effect.

"Wow," he breathes. "Wow."

My heart beats fast. I've never been the kind of girl that guys say *wow* over. Not by a long shot. A part of me still can't believe it.

And then I see the bulge in his pants.

Okay.

Something flips in my brain. I step away from him and give him a twirl, then I follow it up with a little shimmy. He stares at me, fixated. Those dark eyes glowing gold.

"Scout, what are you doing to me?" he groans.

I purse my lips. "You don't like it?"

"You have no idea. But I was just thinking I should take you out for dinner, show you off like you deserve. Meanwhile, my beast—" He breaks off like he can't bring himself to finish the sentence.

"What?" I demand.

"Wants to ravage you again."

I break into a smile. "I don't need showing off, Orion. All I need is you… Well, you and a home cooked meal."

His grin mirrors my own. "Okay, if you say so. To be honest, my beast was getting kinda snarly about letting you out of the house, looking so sexy."

A delicious shiver runs through me. I love how possessive his beast is. And I love how man and beast are at war inside him.

"Well, tell your beast we're staying right here," I say, and at the same moment, I ease the spaghetti straps off my shoulders.

13

Scout

I put my hands on Orion's chest and shove him backward. A smile tugs at his lips and he plays along, falling back on the edge of the bed. He props his weight on his hands and that bulge in his pants gets bigger and bigger.

I have no idea what I'm doing, but I try to remember the songs that my best friend and I used to listen to, and I move in time to the music in my head, raising my arms over my head, then running them over my body.

Orion swallows hard. Holy crap. I feel sexy, power-ful. Gazing deep into his burning eyes, I lay my hands on his shoulders, then slide my knee between his thighs.

Are you really doing this, Scout?

Yes, I am. I'm giving my man a lap dance.

I push that pretty pink bra into his face. He buries

his face in my cleavage with a groan of pure need. He's been sitting on his hands, but now they rise up and cup my ass. I slip onto his lap and grind my lace-clad pussy over his dick. I have no idea if this is what professional laps dancers do, but sheesh, it feels good. I can feel that my panties are soaked already.

"I need to be inside you, baby girl," he growls in my ear, and his voice vibrates all the way through me.

My pussy clenches for him. I need his cock so bad, too.

But I break into a smile. "Not so fast," I whisper.

Then I unzip his jeans and his cock springs out. It's huge, throbbing. Dripping with precum. I slip off his lap and kneeling down, press my lips against it.

"Scout!" he gasps out, like he's surprised. "You don't have to—"

I flick my tongue across the head, and he doesn't finish his sentence. I love tasting him. Salty and sweet; such a turn on. I part my lips and try to take him into my mouth. He's so big, I have to stretch my jaws wide apart, but the sounds that escape his lips are my reward. When I move my lips up and down his shaft, he grasps my hair and his cock starts to move in my mouth, back and forth. *Wow.* So much. It hits the back of my throat, and I try not to gag. I want to make him feel as good as I did when he licked my pussy. After a while I get used to him, and it feels real good the way he's fucking my mouth, sliding in and out. Muttering my name over and over. Tugging on my hair.

"Come here," he rasps at last.

I slide my mouth off his cock and he drags me up,

making me straddle his lap. When my pussy rubs up against his cock, I know what to do. I push my panties aside, and in a second, he's shoving inside me. This monster cock of his is forcing its way through my entrance. It hurts for a second as it pushes through the remnants of my virginity, then it fills me right up. I gasp as it hits home. I'm impaled. He's so deep inside me.

"Fuck," he gasps. "So tight, baby." He grasps my ass in his big hands and starts to move me up and down.

Darn, this feels good. My pussy slides up and down his massive rod, slick with my juices and gripping him tight.

Faster and faster he slams into me. "That's it, ride me, baby," he growls.

I try my best, gripping his shoulders, gazing deep into those golden-glowing eyes, while I ride his monster cock.

He shoves my bra down, freeing my tits.

So good. His cock pounding into me, while he sucks on my aching nipples. An intense feeling wells up in me. My pussy starts to spasm around his girth.

"Look into my eyes, baby," he growls. "I want to see how beautiful you look when you come."

It's hard, because my vision has gone all blurry, but I keep my eyes locked onto Orion's as he thrusts into me. Harder and harder, faster and faster. And it happens.

A beautiful, tingly orgasm rushes through me. One incredible wave after another, starting between my thighs and spreading all over my body. My pussy spasms out of control, and it hasn't quit when Orion stands up with me in his arms. He flips me down on the bed, his cock still buried inside me.

He spreads my thighs wide and starts to thrust hard. He's wild in this position. I sense his beast emerging, and I love it. Love the savage, unrestrained way he fucks me.

His fast, rough rhythm hits my sweet spot, and I come again, and again.

"That's right, baby. Come around my cock," he growls, arching over me, his eyes wild. He plunges into me over and over, and it's like we're in perfect harmony, making sweet, wild music together. I wrap my leg around him, holding him tight, while he drives me wild.

"I'm gonna fill your sweet pussy with my cum," he snarls, and a second later, a roar bursts from his lips and his cock surges. He holds me tight while he ejaculates deep inside me, his hot seed filling me up. Making me his, again and again.

When we collapse at last in a sweaty heap, his face buried in my neck, I gaze up at the ceiling and my eyes tear up. Here I am, my gorgeous mate holding me in his arms, surrounded by all these beautiful things that were made just for me.

I could never have imagined this in my wildest, wildest dreams.

"What is it, baby?" Orion's head jerks up. He gazes into my eyes, frowning, then, with a fingertip, he wipes away the tear that has spilled from my eyes. "Why are you sad?"

"I'm not sad, but how did you know I was crying?"

"My beast sensed it."

"I'm crying because I'm happy. Because I love you."

He breaks into a smile. "Okay, then you can cry," he says solemnly. "But for no other reason. Ever."

I grin. "Nothing can make me sad?"

"Not if I've got anything to do with it," he growls, and presses his soft, lush lips against mine again.

14

Orion

*E*very day I spend with Scout is more wonderful than the last. Seeing her exploring the house brings so much joy to my heart. The smallest thing fills her with so much excitement and gratitude. "But how did you *know?*" she keeps saying, as she discovers one thing after another—

The library, with a spiral staircase leading up to the second level gallery;

The cozy reading alcove that hangs right over the forest, stuffed with comfy cushions;

The collection of vintage teacups and saucers, with a selection of different teas from around the world (all my mom's work; can't take credit for that);

The little maze on the far side of the house, lined

with twinkling fairy lights, and planted with fragrant herbs.

I feel her unfurling, starting to believe that tomorrow is going to be a good day, and the day after that, and the day after that...

"I never want to leave here," she tells me over and over, and that suits me just fine. We spend most of our time in bed, or in the pool, or wandering outside in the sunshine. Part of me is dying to take her out and show her all the good things in the world, but the other part is happy to have her all to myself. There'll be time for all that later. One day soon, I'll take her to meet the clan. I know my mom senses something is up, but so far I've managed to keep her at bay. Truth is, I can't wait for her to meet Scout, either. See the look on her face when she sees that everything turned out just the way she promised. All I needed was to believe in fate and build the perfect nest for my mate.

But for now, I can't get enough of my sweet girl, and I'm not going to let anything get in the way of our time together.

THIS MORNING, the bed is empty when I wake up, though. And I'm disappointed. Every other day, I've woken up first and watched her while she was sleeping. Staring at her beautiful face in a way I couldn't if she was awake, because she'd probably think I was weird. I love to see how her lips always part a little when she's asleep. I love how her eyelids are a little translucent and sometimes I can see her eyes moving back and forth, and I know she's dreaming. She always sleeps sprawled out. She told me her usual bed is a broken old army cot. But here, she relaxes and spreads out like the queen she is.

Often, she throws the covers off, and I can stare at her lovely tits and soft belly. Sometimes I even get a glimpse of the golden triangle of hair between her legs.

But today, her side of the bed is cold.

I jolt upright, sensing that something is wrong.

My beast takes charge and I dash around the house, snuffling, desperate to track her down.

At last, I find her in the floral bedroom—the one I call "Scout's dressing room" now. My heartbeat slows down.

But when she turns to me, I notice that her soft forehead is marred with a frown. Panic jolts through me.

"What is it, honey?"

"Oh, I'm sorry. I couldn't sleep." She swipes the back of her hand across her forehead.

"Something's bothering you. Come tell me about it."

She gives me a brave smile as I draw her down onto the bed and encircle her in my arms.

"Oh, I was just thinking about my family." She puffs out her cheeks. "This is gonna sound real stupid—"

"Scout, nothing you have to say is stupid, trust me." I take hold of her hand and keep stroking it until she's ready to continue.

"I just hate the way that dad is gonna think I failed because I didn't make it back. And I know that's crazy.

I'm so happy here with you. Why should I give a crap what my dad thinks, after the way he treated me?"

I swallow hard. The tears in her eyes are like a knife twisting in my heart.

"You know what I think?" I say carefully. "I think your dad—in his own way—set you an Alpha challenge."

She wrinkles her nose. "What's that?"

"It's common among shifters. When the Alpha of a clan or pack has several sons, he often makes them compete to see who would be best suited to succeed him when he gets old."

She nods thoughtfully. "That figures. He always seems pretty preoccupied about building the community and the family's position in it." She's quiet for a moment, then her expression darkens. "He put me in his Alpha challenge, but he never expected me to make it back."

She springs to her feet, and when I see the fire burning in her eyes, I fall in love with her even more.

"I've got to show him." She paces up and down in front of me. "I can't rest until I do it."

Her small hands are clenched into fists. I reach out and hold them in mine. "You're saying you want to continue with your mission?

She nods fiercely. Then sadness fills her eyes. "I don't know how long it's gonna take. I might be gone for days or even weeks. I can't stand to leave you, Orion, but I've got to do this. I hope you understand."

My heart fills with pride for this tough little girl of mine. She's even more of a fierce she-bear than I knew.

"Okay," I say slowly. "I do understand. And I'll be right here when you get back."

Then I bite back a smile. What *she* doesn't understand is that there's no way I'm leaving her by herself, ever again.

15

Orion

For five whole days, Scout travels through the wilderness, all alone—or so she thinks. Her eyesight and hearing are sharp, so I'm careful to stay well back, but I'm never more than a couple of minutes behind her.

But for my beast, those are two long minutes. Following Scout, not touching her, is agony for my beast. My animal is consumed with possessiveness and jealousy. It's ripping me up inside, howling in pain. This is the only time we'll ever be apart, but it doesn't understand that. It doesn't understand how I can bear to have her so far away from me. She's my mate. There's a tether connecting us, and the farther she is from me, the more my heart hurts.

I wonder if she feels it, too, and I hope she's not suffering.

Every time I catch sight of her slight figure, dressed in the same men's shorts and shirt she arrived in, I have to stop myself from catching her up and making her ride my beast's broad back instead. But I understand how important this mission is for her. She wants to prove to herself—as well as to her father—that she's capable of meeting the challenge. And I know she's gonna make it.

She's so brave, my girl. She keeps her bow handy, and her senses on high alert, but she's not afraid. There's no fear in the intoxicating scent that trails behind her.

Of course, she has no reason to be afraid. Sure, there are a bunch of shifters circling, but most of them know better than to approach a marked female. And the ones that didn't? Well, the bite of my canines was the last thing they ever felt in their miserable lives.

Every night Scout catches a rabbit and roasts it over a campfire with whatever else she's managed to forage. If I had my way, she'd be eating gourmet packed meals, but of course she insisted on going the whole nine yards and hunting all her food. I've just got to keep reminding myself that once this is over, she'll eat like a queen for the rest of her life.

Of course, I help her out as much as I can. If she leaves the campfire to go wash up in the evening, I keep it all built up for her. I catch rabbits and toss them right in her path. And when she's sleeping, curled up in her hammock, I watch over her all night long, making sure her sleeping bag stays tucked up under her chin.

Sometimes, when she finds a secluded spot by the river, she strips off and plunges in. This is the hardest bit for my beast. It darn near goes insane. There she is— my mate, beautiful and vulnerable, her delicious pale body exposed to the wilderness. She doesn't understand how closely she's being watched—and that's probably for the best.

I yearn to go in after her and take her in my arms, claim her once again. It's been too long since I tasted her sweet pussy, sunk my cock deep inside her.

Soon, I tell my beast, desperate to pacify it. It's getting harder to control by the day, more manic and jealous.

By the fifth day, I can see Scout's spirit is tiring. Her feet start to drag, catching on the undergrowth. She's bored of walking, and lonely too, I bet. My heart aches so bad for her.

Just after midday, I pick up a strong scent of humans —at least five of them. Scout starts walking faster and looking around like she recognizes her surroundings.

I fall farther back. Wouldn't put it past these crazy preppers to have rigged up a watchtower.

I hear Scout's fast, anxious breathing as she strides toward a beat-up-looking encampment. Then she stops dead.

Something's wrong.

A gust of wind blows in my direction, and a sickening smell fills my nostrils.

16

Scout

Fuck. What's happened?

I'm back, at long last. After so many days of trekking through the wilderness, my heart aching for my mate.

But something's not right here.

The place looks deserted.

I take off toward our bunker at a run. "Mom? Dad?" I call.

But nobody answers.

I locate the concealed hatch that leads to the bunker, lift it up and climb down the steep flight of steps. There's a terrible smell of vomit. I clap my hand over my mouth to stop myself from puking, too.

"Dad?"

"Scout?"

I stop dead. It's my dad's voice. But he doesn't sound hostile and scathing like he usually does. He sounds... *relieved?*

I dash over to the sleeping area. He's lying on his broken army cot and his face is gray, his skin coated with a greasy sheen.

"Dad!" I yell, my gut twisting. Despite everything, I can't stand to see him like this. "What's happened?"

"Dunno. Think I ate something," he chokes out. "Been sick for two days now."

"Ate what?" I look around the bunker wildly. All the family's food comes in tins or packets, and the use-by dates are probably good until the apocalypse. Either that, or we eat freshly-caught meat.

"Maybe some tuna. One of the tins was weird..." He breaks off with a pained groan. Then he turns his head to puke in the bucket beside his bed.

I swallow hard, fighting the urge to retch.

Okay, I've got this. "Be right back," I tell him. I run to the bathroom, hunt down a cloth and soak it in cold water. I come back and press it to his forehead.

"Thanks, honey." There's something new in the eyes that search mine. "You made it back."

I clench my teeth. I'm not going to get into that now. "Where's mom?" I ask instead.

"She went looking for you all."

I blink. That's not like mom, at all. Does that mean...?

"And Vinny and Owen?"

"Not back yet." He grimaces. He's ashamed. His big strong sons have let him down. I can't help the little flicker of pride that runs through me. I made it back here, all by myself. Yes, I spent a few nights en route, uh, finding my mate, who I'm now missing like crazy, but I navigated the wilderness myself, every step of the way.

I feel heat soaking through the cloth. He's burning up.

"Dad, you've got a fever. Maybe we should get you to—"

There's the sound of a heavy tread behind me. I spin around.

And my heart bounds in joy.

Orion. Right here in the bunker.

I don't hesitate. I just *run* into his arms.

My legs wrap around his waist, my arms loop around his neck, and our lips cling together like we're drowning. A deep rumbling sound comes from his massive chest, and that pain in my own chest disappears. My mate and I are together again. Like two halves of one person. I don't need to ask what he's doing here. I think I knew deep down that he was with me all this time.

It's a long, long time before he lets me down to the ground and gently sets me on my feet. Then he takes my hand in his and together, we turn to my father.

Dad's eyes are bulging so much, they're in danger of dropping right out of his head. He runs his tongue between his dry lips. "W-who's this, Scout?"

"This is my mate, Orion. Orion, meet my dad." I blink, surprised at the way my voice resounds around the room. I hadn't even realized until now that it used to be like a mouse's squeak. Now I sound like a—well, like a confident woman.

A well-loved woman, I think, squeezing Orion's hand.

Of course, you are. More than you know.

What? My head jerks up to meet his gaze. "Did you say something?" I mutter.

A smile tugs at Orion's gorgeous lips.

My soul communicated directly with yours.

I gasp. He definitely didn't speak *those* words out loud. I heard them in my head.

Is this gonna keep happening? I think the sentence real hard.

He grins. *You bet. More and more.*

Wow, well this is all kinds of awesome.

Finally, I remember that someone else is in the room with us.

Dad is looking at us with confusion and something else—like he's figuring out that he's been tricked out of something. "Are you a prepper?" he says hoarsely.

Orion curls his lip. "Nope."

"Where did you two meet?"

"During my mission," I say shortly. I'm not about to let him give me the third degree.

"You're sick." Orion walks over to him and leans forward examining him closely. "What with?"

"He said he ate a weird can of tuna."

"And you've got a high fever, vomiting. Having a hard time speaking?"

"Yup," dad croaks.

"Feel dizzy?"

"Yeah."

"You've probably got botulism," Orion concludes. "You need to go to the hospital."

"No hospitals."

Orion's eyebrows furrow. "Why not?"

"Because they're not going to have them after the Final Fiasco."

Orion's frown gets even deeper. "Is the Final Fiasco coming tomorrow?"

Dad shrugs in that gormless way of his. *Who knows?*

"Probably not, right. So, I think we're good." While Orion scratches his beard thoughtfully, I fight back a grin of delight. No one dares act sarcastic with dad, ever.

"I know you have a vehicle, because Scout told me that you used it to dump her in the wilderness."

I see a muscle in Orion's jaw twitch. I understand how much it's costing him to act civil with my father, and my heart overflows with love for him.

"So, I'm gonna drive you to the nearest ER."

"No way—" Dad starts to say, but his words are cut off by a mighty *roar.*

Orion lays both hands on his own chest, like he's forcing his beast back. "No arguments. You've caused Scout enough misery already. The last thing she needs is you taking yourself out with your own stupidity!"

Tingles run through me. I'm so touched by Orion's protectiveness of me, I could burst.

Orion leans right over my father. "Just one thing I want you to tell me first: Scout won your challenge, yes?"

Dad's lips work silently. "Yup. Yes, she did," he croaks at last.

"So, she's the Alpha now?"

"The what?"

Orion puts his arm around me. "The leader of your clan. Empress of the preppers, whatever you want to call it."

I snigger.

Dad's eyes track back and forth, as if they're moving in time with his brain waves.

"Your two sons haven't made it back yet, have they?"

"No—" Dad gasps and clutches his stomach.

"Scout even took a rest at my place for five whole days, but she still came back first. I think she's stronger than all of you put together."

Dad gives me a long look. "You're right. I've always known it, Scout. That's why I've been so hard on you."

I give a snarl of disgust. "You're a very sad man, dad."

"Say it," Orion presses him. "Tell her she's the Alpha."

"You are, Scout," dad gasps out. "You're the Alpha of us from now on."

I nod nonchalantly. "Okay."

Then Orion hunches over the bed, and suddenly dad is in his arms.

My father who has always been such an overbearing force in my life; a huge, bossy, shouty man. Now he looks so small in Orion's arms. So insignificant.

* * *

WE DROP dad off at the ER, but we don't stay with him. Orion says he wants to track down my mom before nightfall.

"You're so kind," I tell him.

"For you." He kisses my hand. "Anything for you."

I sigh. "I am kinda worried about her."

"I know."

When we get back to the compound, he strips his clothes off and his bear springs out of him.

Of course, he's going to hunt for her as a bear. That makes perfect sense.

Annnd… it looks like I'm riding on his back.

Climb on, baby, his soul tells mine.

I don't hesitate; I take a little run up, and jump right up.

Oh, my gosh, it feels so good to be on his back. Instinctively, my thighs tighten around his broad body, my legs sinking right into his luxurious fur. I lean forward and wrap my arms around his neck.

Sitting comfortably?

You bet.

And we're off.

His bear goes at a trot, keeping its nose close to the ground, and snuffling all the while. I guess it's already on mom's trail.

After an hour or so, he stops.

She's right ahead. Look.

I peer through the branches, not seeing anything.

Probably better if you go on foot for now.

He's got a point. He hunkers down and I slide off his back.

I walk a couple of hundred yards, and there she is—walking slowly, her feet dragging. She's real tired.

A rush of sympathy goes through me and I run after her. "Mom!"

She gasps and turns to face me. "Scout! Thank goodness!" She bursts into tears and throws her arms around me. "Oh, my baby. I thought I'd lost you forever."

"I'm tougher than I look, mom."

"I know you are, honey. But you were all alone. I knew Owen and Vinny would've stuck together."

"Until they were ready to stab each other in the back."

She draws back and gives me a long look. "You're okay?"

"Yeah, I'm fine, mom."

"B-but when did you get back?"

"Earlier today. Look, I need to get you home, but there's something I need to tell you first…"

BY THE TIME we get back to Orion, my mom is *kinda* prepared to be greeted by a giant grizzly bear, but she still lets out a gasp of terror.

I don't blame her. He looks fearsome, all glowing eyes and flashing teeth and claws. And I'm so proud I could cry.

I help her onto his back, and I climb up behind her, and we retrace our steps back to the compound, going a little slower than before.

* * *

WE SPEND THE EVENING TOGETHER. After dropping us off, Orion goes and hunts a couple of rabbits, while mom gets the fire going.

"He's a keeper," she says, when we're alone together.

"I know," I reply happily.

She frowns. "And what good luck that you found each other after your father left you in the wilderness."

"Some might say it's fate," I say, and the mark on the back of my neck—his mark—tingles like crazy.

She gets a dreamy look to her. "He's so big, and strong, and *muscular…*" She finishes with a shiver.

"Mom!" I protest. I don't want to think about my mom having a crush on my mate.

"Oh, I'm sorry. I'm just real happy for you." She squeezes my knee. "I can see he's absolutely crazy about you."

"Really?" I know it's true, but it doesn't hurt to hear it said aloud.

"He can't take his eyes off you."

A thrill goes through me. I love being held in Orion's gaze, so, so much.

"You're gonna make some beautiful babies."

"Mom!" Truth is, I can't wait to have his babies, but there are so many things I want to do first.

"Guess what?" she hisses. "You know that man your father tried to marry you off to?"

"Kinda," I say, and I'm not even joking. Since I first laid eyes on Orion, no other man has meant anything to me.

"Well, he's been round here looking for you. Says he made a big mistake, and he wants you back."

I can't resist a little smile. "And what did you tell him?"

"I said, you only get one chance, buster. And you screwed it up." My mom giggles like a schoolgirl. "Then I told him to get the hell out of here and never come back."

"High five, mom." I hold up my hand and she high-fives me enthusiastically.

I tap a finger against my lips. "Actually, on second thoughts—you think you can get a message out to him, and to all the neighboring prepper families to come here in three days' time?"

"What for?" she leans closer, eyes glittering with excitement. For the first time, I get a glimpse of what she might've been like if she'd married someone other than my father.

"All will be revealed," I say cryptically.

THAT NIGHT, Orion and I go sleep in the forest. There's no way we're staying in the family compound. He clears out a space on the forest floor and makes us a bed out of pine fronds and bracken. I swear it's the comfiest thing I've ever lain on.

Then he strips me bare, and we make love under the stars, just like nature intended.

When I'm finally sated from his attentions, and my eyelids are getting heavy, he shifts into his bear, and wraps me up in his big furry body, and we fall into a deep, blissful sleep together.

Scout

*I*t's another twenty-hour hours before they let dad out of hospital. They diagnosed botulism and malnutrition. He's going to be fine, as long as he keeps taking the bunch of antibiotics they've given him.

He seems different. Quieter. I hope that spending some time out in the normal world has done him good. He thanks Orion and me, shuffling his feet and unable to look us in the eye.

ON OUR SECOND morning in the forest, Orion raises himself up from our bed of bracken and sits, head cocked, frowning.

"What is it?"

"A truck approaching."

"Can't hear anything."

"Just wait…" He listens for a moment. "It's pulled up a couple of hundred yards away. Two guys have gotten out. They're shushing each other. One is saying, "we've gotta look more *tired*, man."

I burst out laughing. "I'll bet a million dollars that's my two brothers. Come on, let's go meet them."

By the time Vinny and Owen emerge from the forest, Orion and I are waiting by the entrance to the compound. When they catch sight of me, they do an identical double take.

"No way?" Owen mutters.

Their gaze drifts to Orion, and their shoulders stiffen at the sight of the much bigger guy.

"Got back days ago," I say cheerfully. "What kept you?"

"We came across a lost hiker. We had to help him get back home," Vinny says.

"Threw us right off course, so we've been walking for days," Owen chips in.

I fold my arms. "That's funny, 'cause we just heard you both getting out of a truck."

Owen gasps in that dramatic, offended way of his. He's been doing it since we were kids. It might've worked on my parents, but it's never worked on me.

"Don't even." Orion steps forward.

My heart gives a little jump. I love how he's just *there* for me. He gives me the space I need to fight my own battles, but I know he's always ready to step in and protect me.

Owen recoils. Then he turns on me, lip curled. "It was *real* hard. How did you get back so quick?"

I shrug. "Guess I'm a pretty good survivalist after all."

* * *

THE THIRD DAY COMES, and I wake up, full of nerves.

"You're gonna be great, baby," Orion murmurs in my ear.

"How did you know I was stressed?"

"Because you're my mate, and I can feel what you feel." He nuzzles my neck.

I close my eyes for a beat, taking strength from him. "Just hope everyone turns up."

"They will. I know your mom's been hard at work."

At eleven-thirty a.m., the first vehicles start to roll in.

There are *a lot* of people. I stay out of sight, but from a distance, I identify all the main prepper families, gathering outside the bunker, gossiping curiously.

"Okay, twelve o'clock, you're ready to roll," Orion says.

I puff out a big breath.

He takes me in his arms and holds me tight. The moment our bodies press together, the slow beat of his big beary heart suffuses me with calm.

"I'll be right here any time you need me, baby," he says. "You're not alone anymore."

"Thank you." I look deep into his eyes, feeling the love flow from him to me and back again. Then I step out from the trees and stride toward the gathering of people, head held high, shoulders back.

"Thank you all for coming," I begin, scanning the familiar and unfamiliar faces. "I called you here to commemorate me winning my father's Alpha challenge."

Everyone looks a little confused.

"A couple of weeks ago, my father dumped us kids in the wilderness, tasking us to make our way back home. I don't think anyone expected me to make it at all—never mind first—but whaddya know? Here I am." I throw my arms wide, and there are a few laughs.

"While I was out in the wilderness, I met my mate—" I indicate Orion. "And I learned a lot from him."

I cast Orion a look. I want him here with me.

He steps up behind me and lays his hands on my shoulders. "Scout accepted the challenge that you presented to her, and she won. Because she's smarter and tougher than the rest of you put together."

From my dad's helpless expression, I can tell that Orion's eyes are boring into him.

"Which makes her your new leader."

My dad's mouth opens, like he's about to say something. Then he drops his head with a conciliatory nod.

"Or, as we say in our world, the Alpha." Orion steps away from me. "Please give a big hand to the new Alpha of the Patterson preppers."

Everyone starts clapping. I can't believe it.

"Scout, is there anything you want to say to mark your first day in new role?"

"Yes." I clasp my hands and step forward, more

confident now. "As Alpha of this family, I decree that no one is going to be forced to live the prepper lifestyle anymore." I focus in on my dad. "Dad, you've chosen to spend your life obsessing over something that's probably never going to happen. Can't you see how miserable that's made you? All of you? Instead of enjoying the days you've been given to the full, you're all looking forward to some shittier days. I mean, seriously, if the apocalypse comes, who cares if you're the only survivors. It's gonna be damn lonely.

"And I get that for some people it's a fun hobby and all, filling up your basements with all that nice stuff, but come on, people, live a little!"

I stop talking and a long silence rings out.

Then a small voice from the crowd goes, "yeah!"

Then someone claps.

And someone else.

Suddenly, around half the congregation is clapping and cheering.

Not dad, of course. That would be a giant leap.

But all these people. Who actually hate living this darn wretched lifestyle.

My mom slinks up to me with tears in her eyes. "Well done, honey," she murmurs and throws her arms around me.

Then Owen and Vinny come up, too. "Great work, little sis," Vinny says. "You've got the balls to say what no one else dared to."

"The ovaries, thank you," I say primly, but inside I'm glowing.

I close my eyes for a beat. They haven't been the

kind of big brothers a girl could wish for, but they didn't exactly have a good role model to set them on the right track in life.

"C'mere." I beckon to them. "Let's be friends instead of adversaries, huh?" I say, and I pull them all into a group hug.

Owen draws back. "How about I go get some beers?"

"Coming with you," Vinny replies, and the two of them hare off.

They're back soon, and the party kicks off. Alcohol and music have been banned since we came to live in the forest—and by the looks of it, in most prepper households, because everyone is partying like its 2099.

Everyone except for that loser who rejected me. He's standing behind a tree, but I feel his eyes burning into me. I can do that now I've connected with my bear mate. I'm much more aware of my surroundings than I used to be.

"What the fuck?" Orion growls, evidently noticing him at the same moment.

I go to catch his arm, then I stop myself. Remembering the curl of that prick's lip when he rejected me.

A moment later, Orion's got him in a chokehold, and he's beckoning me over.

"This is Derek," he tells me. "He thinks he has some claim on you. Or he *did*."

I glance at Derek, whose face has turned purple. I frown. "Until you tried to choke the life out of him?"

"Yup," Orion says cheerfully, and I notice that his canines are longer than usual. His bear is having a good time.

"No, he never had a claim on me," I say, smiling pleasantly. "But he did reject my father's offer to sell him my *purity*."

"He *what!?*" Orion roars.

"I-I was freaked out, that's all," Derek chokes out. "He fucking surprised me, turning up on the doorstep like that. I didn't know what to say."

"Not exactly how I remember it," I say, curling my lip right back at him.

"You looked real different then, Scout."

"You rejected my girl?" Orion snarls.

"I-I didn't *reject* her. I mean, look at her, she's fucking hot—"

A bellow of rage pours from Orion's throat.

I shake my head sadly. "Wrong answer, doofus."

Then I turn on my heel and leave them to it.

I'M CHATTING to one of the prepper teens when Orion saunters back a few minutes later, hands in his pockets.

"Everything okay?" I say.

"Yup." He shrugs.

"You didn't do anything…?"

"Just sent him home with a piece of my mind." He cracks open a beer and hands it to me.

I slide him a sideways glance. I could interrogate him some more. But the truth is, I don't need to hear anything else. Orion protected me, and that's all I need to know.

I tip the beer back and take my first ever sip.

Urggh. I shudder at the bitter taste.

He laughs. "Might take some getting used to."

"Think I'll stick with soda," I say. Then I think of all those cans of soda he stocked in his fridge, just for me. "Gosh, I miss our place," I blurt out.

Tenderness glows in his eyes, and he strokes my cheek. "I was just thinking the same thing. You about ready to leave?"

I look around. Dad is drinking beer, and busting moves from some best-forgotten era. A bunch of other strait-laced parents look like they're already as drunk as skunks.

"Sure am."

Orion takes a cell phone out of his pocket and starts typing. "Hang tight for fifteen minutes."

I don't ask why. These days I'm starting to love surprises—ever since he taught me that a surprise doesn't mean a giant asteroid plummeting toward the earth. It can be something good, too.

WE WATCH the party for a little while longer, then Orion grabs my hand. "Okay, let's go."

I look for my mom, tell her we're leaving, and we sneak out, laughing joyously.

In the clearing is a shiny red truck, and standing in front of it is a tall, broad-shouldered woman.

She has the same big dark eyes and thick wavy hair as Orion.

His mom.

My gut tightens. I've been nervous to meet her, worried she'll be disappointed.

But she rushes toward me and grasps my hands in hers. "My dear, you're *The One.*"

"Are you sure?" I blurt out.

She laughs. "I've never been surer of anything. And I've been waiting *so* long to meet you."

She introduces herself as Nora, but says to feel free to call her mom, or whatever I feel most comfortable with, and insists that I sit beside her in the front passenger seat.

"Mom's just gonna drop us off today," Orion says pointedly. "She's got somewhere she needs to be later."

"That's right, honeybun, but we'll have plenty of time to chat during the journey, don't you worry." She gives Orion a big, cartoonish wink.

She's as good as her word. It takes a couple of hours to get back to Orion's house, and by the time we arrive, I swear Nora knows every last thing about me. Apparently, I'm *exactly like* the image she got from The Fates. I tell her how much I love the house and all the little touches she thought of, and she exclaims in delight. She's adorable. I see how much she loves Orion, and how happy she is that he's found his mate at last.

She takes a narrow turn off the main road and we pass through a confusing network of dirt tracks, but when we're a few hundred feet from the house, I *know*. I don't know how; I just sense it in my bones. It's a feeling of yearning, of finding my place in the world.

We take one final turn and the house swings into view. I gasp. It's even more breathtaking than I remember. All flashing glass panels, clean lines, and that welcoming blue-green glow.

Orion jumps out and hugs Nora. "Thanks so much, mom," he says. "Can we invite you for dinner tomorrow?"

"Oh, you'd better!" she pinches his cheek. Then she turns and pulls me into another long hug. "Such a pleasure to meet you, my dear. I can't wait to see you again tomorrow."

"Me too!" I say. "I might even manage to cook something nice in that amazing kitchen."

"Your mom is so great," I tell Orion as she drives off.

"Yeah, she's pretty cool," he says, grinning. "Sorry for the third degree though. She was just real excited to meet you."

"Oh, same here. I can't believe how much she knows about me already."

"She's spooky like that. You better get used to it." He puts his arm around my shoulder. "Now, let's go home, my beautiful mate."

It feels different now. Last time I was here, I had this nagging sense of unfinished business. But now, all that's behind us, and I know nothing is going to come between us again.

I stop walking as something occurs to me. "You know something?" I say. "The first time I came here I was unconscious?"

He crooks one of his thick eyebrows. "Sure do. I had to carry you in my arms." He lunges for me, and the next thing I know, he's tossing me over one of his broad shoulders.

"Oh, my god, you carried me like *this*?" I squeak, from my upside-down position.

"Nope. You weren't my mate then. And, I was kinda worried about you."

"Is this how a bear carries his mate?"

"Oh, yeah," he growls and swats my ass.

Heat surges through my core. Is it wrong that I like being carried around caveman style?

Whatever, I don't care. All I want to do is get indoors, get out of our clothes, and have my big grizzly mate claim me, all night long.

EPILOGUE

Six months later

"Oh, my god, I think I'm going to be sick."

"That's okay." Orion smoothes my hair back from my forehead and speaks softly into my ear. "If you've gotta puke, you've gotta puke."

I giggle, and instantly my stomach quits churning. "Would you still love me if I puked all over the beautiful new laptop you've bought me?"

"Baby, I'd love you if you puked over a hundred laptops. Now, as much as I'm enjoying this topic of conversation, shall we check your results?"

"I've so failed," I moan.

"You worked super hard. You got great scores in all the practice questions. You're the smartest person I've ever met. If somehow that didn't all align when you took your test, you can just do it again. It's nothing to worry about."

With every sentence, my heartbeat slows. Orion knows how to calm me like no one else.

There's nothing to worry about.

The bottomless dread that consumed me throughout my childhood has *almost* disappeared under his care and easygoing nature.

I hold my breath and, keeping my eyes half-closed, I jab at my laptop's trackpad.

"798!" Orion hollers, before I've even absorbed the blurry figures in front of me. He plants a smacking kiss on my cheek. Then he lifts me right up, holding me up high with his massive arms and spinning me around. "Baby, you did it! An almost perfect score!"

"Oh, my god!" I say over and over. "I've got my GED!"

"The world is your oyster!"

I laugh joyously, beyond touched at how excited Orion is for me. Ever since I told him how it bothered me that I hadn't graduated high school, he's been encouraging me.

Unsurprisingly, there were a lot of gaps in my parents' "home-schooling" syllabus, so for the past three months I've been studying my ass off. And it's finally paid off.

"And all because of you." I wrap my legs around his waist and kiss him, but he pulls back.

He taps my chest with his fingertip. "No, Scout, all because of you."

"Okay, well, a bit because of me."

"So, what's next?" he says. "College? An internship?"

I bite my lip. I've refused to think about any of this stuff until I got my GED, because I was worried it would jinx it. Then I gaze over the terrace rail at the morning sunshine illuminating the forest—our forest. "I don't think I want to leave here," I say.

He frowns. "We'll come back for college vacations. But now's your time to go out into the world. Enjoy all that stuff you've been missing out on."

I sigh. It's funny—since I met my mate, I haven't felt like I'm missing anything. We spend a lot of time here, in our amazing house. The rest of the time, we hang out with his awesome clan in their territory, and I couldn't be happier.

"Okay, we're going out for a celebration dinner tonight. Somewhere fancy. Cocktails first."

I grin. He's a big ol' grizzly, and his beast is happiest when it's in the forest. Hell, it could probably spend the rest of its life there. But he always makes sure to take me out and show me a good time.

"Okay. If you insist. Maybe I'll wear my new dress."

A sound escapes his lips. He coughs to cover it, but he's not quick enough. I hear his bear's possessive growl. My new dress *is* kinda skimpy. It has a plunging neckline and cut outs on the sides.

"Good idea," he chokes out.

My grin gets wider. "But won't your bear be riled up all night?" I say innocently.

He shakes his head, and his eyes get that tell-tale glow. "Not if we tire it out first."

"And how are we gonna do that?" I put my fingertip in my mouth and suck it.

"Jesus, Scout," he groans. A second later, he's tearing my T-shirt off. It's the only thing I'm wearing, and now I'm stark naked, bathed by the warm sunshine.

Orion stares at me, a growl of pure desire pouring from his lips. Every time, it's like the first time. He makes me feel like the most desirable woman in the world.

He's not wearing anything, of course, and his cock is already rock hard and ready for me.

At the sight of it, my pussy starts to throb, and I feel moisture pooling at the tops of my thighs.

He flips me around and walks me over to the edge of the terrace. A moment later, he's pressing the head of his cock to my soaking wet entrance.

I love the way Orion touches me and goes down on me with his amazing tongue. But sometimes, there's no foreplay required.

Sometimes, all I need is to bend over the terrace rail and have my big, grizzly mate take me from behind.

EPILOGUE

Eight years later

"Where are you?" Castor asks. My five-year-old son is lying on his back, little hands cushioning his head while he stares up at a perfect starry night.

"You see that cluster of stars over there?" Orion points to three bright stars aligned in a row. "That's Orion's belt. That's where he carried his weapons as he roamed the skies."

"And where's mom?"

"You see those stars that form a V-shape? They're real faint because they're far away."

"I see them!" Castor exclaims, as he does every time we have this conversation. Which is once a week at least.

"Well, that's the Pisces constellation. Two fish connected together."

"And where are we?" Pollux, my other five-year-old son shrills. He's standing up, hands shoved in the pocket of his pajamas, mouth open in wonder.

"You see those two bright stars, with those lines of smaller stars coming off them? That's you, and that's your brother."

"Wow," they say in unison. "Wow."

My heart swells. This is their favorite bedtime story, more than any book. Every time there's a clear night, Orion and I bring them outside and point out all the constellations, and tell the story of how we met, and they're amazed anew.

"Okay, time for bed, my heavenly twins." I kiss each of them on top of their dark heads. There are groans of protest, but when Orion crouches down and helps them clamber onto his back, they cling on like baby monkeys, shrieking in excitement.

Once we've gone through the bedtime routine and they're sound asleep in their bunkbeds, Orion and I come back outside. It's a beautiful spring night and the air is full of the rich smells of the forest.

We lay back on a soft blanket and I snuggle into my mate's arms.

"How's our latest constellation?" Orion strokes the swell of my belly.

I shoot him a dark look. Since our first cubs turned out to be twins, born under the sign of Gemini, Orion thinks it's a sign that we're going to have one cub for each sign of the zodiac. Our three-year old daughter,

April, an Aries, is asleep upstairs, and this one is going to be a Cancerian. But no way am I giving birth another ten times. Six kids is my absolute max.

"*Our baby* is very much awake," I say. "Think she can't wait to meet her brothers."

He nuzzles me. "You know how sexy it is when you get sassy with me?"

"Nope?" I say innocently.

"Mmm… very." He slides his hand between my thighs.

I bite back a moan as the familiar heat floods through me. Eight years mated to Orion, and all it takes to get me wet is a kiss or a caress.

A moment later, he's arching over me, keeping his weight off my big belly while he kisses me deeply. His fingers are deft as he unbuttons my dress and eases off my bra, and once again, I'm naked under the stars. "So beautiful, Scout," he murmurs as he dips his head to my big, swollen breasts and kisses them all over. Eight years together and he still worships my body like it's the first time. Doesn't matter whether I'm pregnant, or I've just given birth, he can't get enough of me.

He slips behind me and spoons me, his big cock pushing its way into me, filling me up so perfectly. He fucks me slow and smooth, telling me how much he loves me in his growly, sexy voice. And when he tips me right over the edge, it feels like the stars are falling from the sky, showering us with their blessings.

THE END

READ THE OTHER BOOKS IN THE SERIES

If you like fated-mate romances, with plenty of V-card fun and tons of feels, check out the other books in the series at:

arianahawkes.com/obsessed-mountain-mates

READ MY OTHER OBSESSED MATES SERIES

If you like steamy insta-love romance, featuring obsessed, growly heroes who'll do anything for their mates, check out my Obsessed Mates series. All books are standalone and can be read in any order.

Get started at arianahawkes.com/obsessed-mates

READ THE REST OF MY CATALOGUE

MateMatch Outcasts: a matchmaking agency for beasts, and the women tough enough to love them.

★★★★★ "A super **exciting, funny, thrilling, suspenseful and steamy shifter romance series**. The characters jump right off the page!"

★★★★★ "**Absolutely Freaking Fantastic**. I loved every single word of this story. It is so full of **exciting twists that will keep you guessing until the very end** of this book. I can't wait to see what might happen next in this series."

Ragtown is a small former ghost town in the mountains, populated by outcast shifters. It's a secretive place, closed-off to the outside world - until someone sets up a secret mail-order bride service that introduces women looking for their mates.

Get started at arianahawkes.com/matematch-outcasts

CONNECT WITH ME

If you'd like to be notified about new releases, giveaways and special promotions, you can sign up to my mailing list at arianahawkes.com/mailinglist. You can also follow me on BookBub and Amazon at:

bookbub.com/authors/ariana-hawkes
amazon.com/author/arianahawkes

Thanks again for reading – and for all your support!

Yours,
Ariana

* * *

USA Today bestselling author Ariana Hawkes writes spicy romantic stories with lovable characters, plenty of suspense, and a whole lot of laughs. She told her first story at the age of four, and has been writing ever since, for both work and pleasure. She lives in Massachusetts with her husband and two huskies.

www.arianahawkes.com

GET TWO FREE BOOKS

Join my mailing list and get two free books.

Once Bitten Twice Smitten

A 4.5-star rated, comedy romance featuring one kickass roller derby chick, two scorching-hot Alphas, and the naughty nip that changed their lives forever.

Lost To The Bear

He can't remember who he is. Until he meets the woman he'll never forget.

Get your free books at arianahawkes.com/freebook

READING GUIDE TO ALL OF MY BOOKS

Obsessed Mates

Her River God Wolf

Her Biker Wolf

Her Alpha Neighbor Wolf

Her Bad Boy Trucker Wolf

Her Second Chance Wolf

Her Convict Wolf

Obsessed Mountain Mates

Driven Wild By The Grizzly

Snowed In With The Grizzly

Chosen By The Grizzly

Off-Limits To The Grizzly

Taken Home By The Grizzly

Fated To The Grizzly

Shifter Dating App Romances

Shiftr: Swipe Left for Love 1: Lauren

Shiftr: Swipe Left for Love 2: Dina

Shiftr: Swipe Left for Love 3: Kristin

Shiftr: Swipe Left for Love 4: Melissa

Shiftr: Swipe Left for Love 5: Andrea

Shiftr: Swipe Left for Love 6: Lori

Standalone releases

Tiger's Territory

Shifter Holiday Romances

Bear My Holiday Hero

Ultimate Bear Christmas Magic Boxed Set Vol. 1

Ultimate Bear Christmas Magic Boxed Set Vol. 2

Made in United States
Troutdale, OR
08/31/2024

22467780R00086